KU-361-172

The Bold Enchanter

'Ah, my dear,' answered the Enchanter with a thin smile, 'dreams can be very deceptive, you know.'

The Bold Enchanter is the one behind all the mischief. When the spells on Earth go wrong, and the wrong kind of magic is unleashed, Tom and Eleanor are the only ones who can save the kingdom. The Queen's wish for Magic and Mystery brought much more than she bargained for, and now someone has to sort it out. But that means many adventures and, somehow, Tom and Eleanor have to find their way to the moon.

The moon, of course, really is made of cheese—Edam, Stilton, every kind of cheese that you can think of. They have to cross the moon cheesescape of boiling Fondue and craggy Cheddar to face the Bold Enchanter in his own castle. Will they win? And what will it all be like when they get home again?

Weem Whitaker spent his childhood in rural North Yorkshire before going to Cambridge to read Classics. After doing research in ancient philosophy, he moved back to the hamlet where he grew up, and now lives there with his wife. He enjoys walking in the local countryside, which provides part of the inspiration for his writing. *The Bold Enchanter* is his second novel.

GALWAY COUNTY LIBRARIES
WITHDRAWN FROM CIRCULATION

The Bold Enchanter

ALSO BY WEEM WHITAKER

The Alchemy Set

The Bold Enchanter

Weem Whitaker

GALWAY COUNTY LIBRARIES

OXFORD
UNIVERSITY PRESS

OXFORD

UNIVERSITY PRESS

Great Clarendon Street, Oxford OX2 6DP

Oxford University Press is a department of the University of Oxford.
It furthers the University's objective of excellence in resarch, scholarship,
and education by publishing worldwide in

Oxford New York
Athens Auckland Bangkok Bogota Buenos Aires Calcutta
Cape Town Chennai Dar es Salaam Delhi Florence Hong Kong Istanbul
Karachi Kuala Lumpur Madrid Melbourne Mexico City Mumbai
Nairobi Paris São Paulo Singapore Taipei Tokyo Toronto Warsaw

and associated companies in Berlin Ibadan

Oxford is a registered trade mark of Oxford University Press
in the UK and in certain other countries

Copyright © Weem Whitaker 1999

The moral rights of the author have been asserted

First published in 1999

All rights reserved. No part of this publication may be reproduced,
stored in a retrieval system, or transmitted, in any form or by any means,
without the prior permission in writing of Oxford University Press.
Within the U.K., exceptions are allowed in respect of any fair
dealing for the purpose of research or private study, or criticism or
review, as permitted under the Copyright, Designs and Patents Act 1988,
or in the case of reprographic reproduction in accordance with
the terms of the licences issued by the Copyright Licensing Agency.
Enquiries concerning reproduction outside these terms and in other
countries should be sent to the Rights Department, Oxford University Press,
at the above address.

This book is sold subject to the condition that it shall not, by way of trade or
otherwise, be lent, re-sold, hired out or otherwise circulated without
the publisher's prior consent in any form of binding or cover other than that in
which it is published and without a similar condition including this condition
being imposed on the subsequent purchaser

British Library Cataloguing in Publication Data available

ISBN 0 19 271759 6

Printed and bound in Great Britain by
Biddles Ltd, Guildford and King's Lynn

J137, 710
€ 8.84

For Katie

Contents

CHAPTER I

GALWAY COUNTY LIBRARIES

The Wish

It was a dark November day. Roaring gusts of wind shook the woods, driving sudden squalls of rain against the leafless trees. Where the valley was narrowest, the swollen river churned down a series of falls, and nearby there stood a mill.

Tom, the miller's son, was carrying sacks of grain out from the storehouse to be ground into flour, setting his face against the wind as the dead leaves flew up around him in swirls.

'That's enough for today,' said the miller, coming out to meet him. 'I'll work grinding flour in this damp, with scarce light enough to see by, and worse weather coming, by my reckoning.'

Tom dropped the sack he was carrying in the mill, and the pair of them stood outside and sniffed the air. The trees were wailing in the wind, while the river foamed angrily past the crags, then leapt down the falls to a deep, surging pool below.

Then Tom heard the note of a horn. Across the other side of the valley a file of horsemen was making its way along a narrow path where the ground rose up steeply from the river.

'It's the Royal hunting-party,' said Tom. 'They say they're out after that savage boar that lives deep in the woods.'

'I'd rather have my job than theirs,' said the miller. 'To be out on this sort of a day! And with danger in it, besides.' He shook his head, and went back into the mill, followed by his son.

There were those in the hunting-party who shared the miller's opinion.

'I can't think what made you want to come out on a day like this,' said the Princess Eleanor to her mother.

'Oh, Eleanor!' the Queen reproached her. 'This is *fun*. Anything might happen. It's an adventure.'

The King turned in his saddle. 'Don't be *too* adventurous, my dear. If anyone falls into that river, it will be the end of them.'

Soon they left the cliff path behind, and the ground flattened out. They had come to the maze of thickets and glades haunted by the terrible boar. Everyone began thrashing the bushes for some sign of the beast, and the Queen spurred forward into the gloom.

'Shouldn't we stick with the others?' Princess Eleanor asked, catching her up.

'Nonsense! We want to be the first ones to see the boar, don't we?'

'Yes, but—'

At that moment the rain came on in earnest. It swept through the woods like a torrent and hissed on the leaves underfoot, until the whole world seemed made of water.

The Queen sat up and listened. 'Wasn't that the horn?'

'I don't think so.'

'It was! It came from down that slope!'

'Mother, wait—'

But the Queen was off, slithering down the muddy bank that led to the river. Eleanor followed, keeping her horse on its feet with difficulty, and dismounted beside her mother. The Queen held up her hand, and Eleanor listened. First there was only the wild rushing of the river and the driving rain. And then she heard it too: a high, thin note, like a song, beautiful but urgent.

'It's coming from the river!' the Queen cried. Before Eleanor could stop her, she had seized up a dead branch, and was sliding down the mud to the very edge of the torrent.

'*Please* come back! You'll drown!'

Eleanor followed her mother's eye, and there, swiftly carried along through the dark, seething water, was a point of light. The Queen threw out her branch, teetered over the edge, and pulled it in. There, clinging on the end of the branch, was a glowing human creature.

Eleanor helped pull her mother back up the bank, and the Queen sank to the ground, out of breath. Her eyes were almost starting out of her head.

'Eleanor, look!' she whispered. 'It's the Lady of the Woods!'

Eleanor looked, and she saw: a tiny, green-clad thing, with a glow of light hovering all round her: the fabled Lady of the Woods, often spoken of, but never seen.

'You have saved me from death,' said the Lady. 'Every creature has its element, where it belongs and has its power, and mine is the air. In the water I have less strength than a child.'

The Queen leant forward, staring, while the Lady of the Woods took a tiny ring from her finger.

'This is my gift to you,' she said. 'In this ring there is a wish. When you have decided on something you truly want, and cannot obtain in any other way, then tell it to the ring. The wish in it will come to me, and I shall do what I can to make you happy. Choose well.'

'Oh, I shall . . . I shall,' breathed the Queen, and the Lady of the Woods tossed her the ring. It grew as it came, and by the time it landed in the Queen's hand it was a perfect fit for her finger. And then the Lady was gone, a bright speck flying off into the gloom of the woods.

'Well!' whispered the Queen, admiring the ring on her finger. 'Well!'

And then they both heard the note of the horn, and Eleanor had to drag her mother away from the river bank and back up to the thicket where they had left the main party. The boar had got away. Dusk was beginning to fall, and the King had decided it was time to return to the Castle.

On the way home the Queen told everyone her story. 'And,' she finished up, 'the *really* exciting part is still to come. How do you think I'll use the Wish?'

Over the next months the Queen strained as hard as she could to find an answer. She sat and thought, and her ladies-in-waiting sat and thought, and they had all sorts of ideas, each one of which she wrote down in a notebook, discussed, argued for and against, and finally crossed out.

By the time June came, the Queen had almost given up. Late one sunny afternoon she was sitting in the topmost room of the Great Tower with her ladies-in-waiting, while Princess Eleanor sat in a window seat reading a book.

'It's no use,' the Queen sighed, looking down the crossed-out list of ideas. 'New coach, new dress, new jewels, new crown . . . There's really no point. I've got everything I want already.'

Princess Eleanor looked up from her book. 'Why don't you save it up? One day there's bound to be something you really need.'

'But I can't bear just to leave it sitting there,' the Queen moaned. 'I've got to use it.'

'Well, choose something then. Come on, mother.

You've been fussing over it for six whole months. You've stopped enjoying the things you *have* got.'

'Eleanor, I can't just throw it *away*. I've got to choose carefully. Come on, everyone. Think! There must be *something* I don't have.'

The three ladies-in-waiting creased their brows.

'How about a grand banquet?' Lady Linda suggested.

'We have far too many banquets as it is.'

'I'd wish for a husband,' said Lady Clara, after a pause.

'Really, Lady Clara! I'm already married.'

'I think if it were me,' began Lady Samantha dreamily, 'I'd wish to see the Lady of the Woods, just like happened to you. That's a sight most people never see in their whole lives.'

'Your Majesty was very, very lucky,' agreed Lady Linda.

The Queen sighed, remembering. 'It's true. It was magical—just magical.'

'They say there were once goblins in the woods,' Lady Samantha went on, 'and there are stories of sprites and spooks; perhaps someone's grandfather saw one once, in an old house, at some special time of the year. But I've never seen anything like that, and I don't know anyone who has.'

'And magic,' put in Lady Clara. 'Who ever sees any of that? Now, Your Majesty saw a real piece of magic, when that ring grew in mid-air to fit your finger. I wish I'd seen it.'

'Still, this isn't helping us to choose a wish,' said Lady Linda briskly. 'Let's all think as hard as we can, and maybe we'll have an idea.'

The three ladies-in-waiting frowned up at the ceiling or down at the floor; but a broad smile was creeping over the Queen's face, and then she whispered, 'I've got it!'

The three ladies jumped.

'What?' they all asked at once, and Eleanor looked up anxiously from her book.

'I've got all that money can buy,' breathed the Queen. 'A kingdom, a castle, clothes, coaches, jewels . . . But what I don't have is magic—Magic and Mystery!'

'Oh, Your Majesty!' Lady Clara cooed.

'There's magic hiding all around us!' the Queen went on. 'Elves and enchantments and wizardry and spells— They're there, I know it, though no one ever sees them. But I'm going to see them all! Now for the ring, and Magic and Mystery!'

The Queen was already past her ladies and on the way to the door. Eleanor threw down her book and jumped up. 'Now wait a minute, mother. Just sit down and think about it. What *sort* of Magic and Mystery?'

'Any sort. Every sort. I don't care!'

She was springing down the steps of the spiral staircase now, with her ladies after her, and they were moaning with excitement now too.

'Mother, please!' Princess Eleanor begged from behind. '*Anything* might happen!'

'I mean it to!' shouted the Queen, bursting from the bottom of the staircase into the next room.

'Spooks and Pixies!' panted Lady Linda, following the Queen through the Long Gallery.

'Spells and Enchantments,' added Lady Clara.

'Ghosts and Goblins!' concluded Lady Samantha.

'Wait and see!' replied the Queen, and swept into her bedchamber. 'Now, where is it?' And she began tipping out her jewel boxes all over the floor.

Eleanor watched her in desperation. 'But are you sure that sort of thing's what you want?'

'It must be: I've got everything else.' The Queen closed

a small casket with a snap, and looked around the room, now littered with brooches, trinkets, and rings. Then her eye fell on the great marquetry chest, and she began pulling out its drawers, first the obvious ones and then the secret ones.

'But . . . ' Eleanor made one more try. 'It's so vague!'

'Don't care! Magic—ring—Mystery—Wish . . . Aah!' The Queen pulled open the last drawer and lifted out of it a ring—pure gold, with a flawless sapphire set in it, as blue as the sky. She held it up to the evening sun, gazing at it as if trying to see the wish hidden inside, and then she put it on her finger.

'I wish,' said the Queen, 'for Magic and Mystery!'

The ring shuddered, and deep within its sky-blue heart something moved, like an eagle soaring almost out of sight on a still day. Then, with a sudden shock, the wish burst out of the stone like a salmon jumping from the water.

'Magic and Mystery!' The words rang out, as the Wish, imprisoned so long, spoke its message and flew off round the room. Three times it circled the chamber, like a trapped swallow, and whispered three times in the ear of each of them. Then it was off, through the open window and out into the calm June evening.

Down among the roofs of the town it flew, between chimneys and steep overhanging gables, and on through the market-place; and all the time it kept repeating the message that was its being. Some folk who were walking home through the emptying streets looked up in surprise, but the Wish passed on, beyond the last house and out into the dusty highroad, speeding west in the golden light of the evening.

'Magic and Mystery! Magic and Mystery!' On it flew, and in the last village before the woods it turned sharply down a lane past an inn with a great eagle over its door, carved in oak. It swished past the innkeeper, on down to the river, then turned and sped upstream. Low it skimmed, round one bend and another, now into deep shade as it entered the woods and the banks rose higher. Here it came to ancient woodland, the true home of magic, where twisted trees came tangling down to the water, crouching under the crags.

There, by the still pool below the falls, Tom, the miller's son, was sitting on the bank fishing. He looked up. The birds had stopped singing, and something shot past upstream, flying low like a kingfisher, bringing a whisper of words that hung in the air and was gone.

Higher and higher, up into the wildest parts of the hills the Wish flew, where the woods were a maze of knolls and glades, and stunted trees clung among the crags. Up it bounded from rock to rock beside a rushing stream, until at last it came out on a high hilltop.

Here stood an oak, old, stooping, and bent. From one of its branches there hung a thing which looked like a bees' nest, but the Wish knew well enough what it was. Whatever its form, the Wish would always know the home of the Lady of the Woods.

The Wish alighted at the door, still repeating its message. An elf who was keeping guard jumped, and hurried off inside. The honeycombed labyrinth led him at last to the room where the Lady sat, weaving spells in a green-gold glow.

'A Wish has come, my Lady.'

The Lady of the Woods looked up from the pile of finished spells by her side, and nodded gently. The Wish burst straight in past the elf, and hovered in the air before the Lady.

'Magic and Mystery! Magic and Mystery!'

The Lady of the Woods looked at it and raised her eyebrows. 'You have come from the Queen, I think.'

'Magic and Mystery!'

'An unexpected choice. But we must do all we can to make the Queen happy, and I think I can say that she will not be disappointed. Now,' she said, turning to the elf, 'first take this wish and put it with the others. Then bring me my wand and my Book of Wonders, and fetch me nine new sacks of elf-seed to sow, elves of wisdom, elves of whimsy, dancing elves, poetic elves, elves of magic, elves of music, elves hard-working and elves helpful, and elves of reverie and daydream. Then wake me nine of the most fantastic dreams we have, and bring me my Golden Horn.'

The house stirred into activity, and the Wish was led off to join its new companions: and so Magic and Mystery went to lie beside Wealth beyond the Dreams of Avarice, The Princess's Hand in Marriage, and a great many others. The elves returned, bringing this item and that, and all was loaded on the Lady's carriage, hovering ready by the door.

Then the Lady of the Woods rose from her weaving and seated herself in her carriage. The two dragonflies hummed in their harness; their wings flashed and the sun glinted on the blue of their bodies. Then the elf-coachman touched them with the whip, and the coach leapt into the air.

Down into the woods they flew, where the setting sun shed a light more golden and mysterious than ever. Nothing looked like itself. The blue of the river was a richly dyed carpet leading into some great hall, while the trees on either side were pillars of grey marble holding up a domed ceiling of leaves, patterned in gold and green. Through it the carriage swept, and the Lady scattered the elf-seed from her nine sacks on this side and that, touching each handful with her wand; and the seed caught the sunlight as it fell.

On the highest tree in the forest the coach came to rest, and the Lady of the Woods took out her Golden Horn, touched it with her wand and blew a long note, which floated down into every recess of the woods and hills. And then a rustling and a stirring began. The echoes woke in the rocks, the trees unbent, and all the strange things that were normally deep asleep, well hidden away, started to yawn and stretch themselves, and consider that it was time to come out and be seen.

The carriage flew on, and now the Lady of the Woods shook the dreams and woke them from their doze, tapped them with her wand, and sent them flying slowly off to cling to some tree, waiting for the darkness. They were drowsy things by day, but already they could sense the coming of night, and soon they would be wide awake, ready to guide some sleeper to a strange and unimagined land.

The sun was setting. The coach sped on, out of the woods, over villages and fields; and everywhere was the glint of the elf-seed as it fell, and everywhere sounded the clear note of the Golden Horn. Down over the town she flew, the seed settling gently between the roofs and down the chimneys, down even to the narrowest alley and the deepest cellar. Then to the Castle, through the very window of the Queen's bedchamber, and up to the top of the Great Tower: and there she drew out her horn for the last time.

Its pure note drifted over the Castle and the town below, and once again there was the gentle stirring of strange hidden things. People never know what invisible creatures there are asleep under their noses; it might be

10

that in an old house some ancient thing has crept up on top of a cupboard and slowly faded away and forgotten itself; or perhaps an old ghost becomes tired, appears less often, and begins to melt into nothingness. Other creatures there are that are shy, and need to be called out by a bold summons; and there are everyday things too, chairs and clocks and gloves and shoes, which we never suspect of having a will of their own, until they are reminded of it by the right sort of magic. All these now began to stir, and both town and Castle were filled with a creaking and a sighing.

'Only one more task,' said the Lady to her coachman. 'Back to the woods!'

The elf cracked his whip, and the dragonflies shot forward. Over town and fields, back to the wilds they flew, and alighted in a great clearing in the very heart of the forest. Here among long, eerie tree-shadows the Lady of the Woods got out her Book of Wonders. She set it on the ground and touched her wand to it, and the book began to grow. Up and up it rose, until a fully-sized man could have sheltered in its pages; and then a cold wind blew from it, a flurry of dead leaves shot out, and the giant pages flapped to and fro.

The Lady of the Woods smiled. There was a world of legends and wonders in that book, and her magic had opened a door between that strange, wild place, and the sleepy sunlit clearing. Now there came a wailing, and a whistling, and then a hollow bellowing, and a rush of creatures burst from the book and scattered into the forest, too quick to be seen.

Again the cold wind blew and the pages flapped, and this time a knight in full armour galloped out, then another and another, their lances levelled for the charge, their armour gleaming bronze in the setting sun. The ground shook, and in a moment they were gone too, intent on the beasts that were only a step ahead of them.

'Five, six, seven,' the Lady of the Woods counted. 'Where are the last two? Have I miscounted?'

'I counted seven too, my Lady,' the coachman said.

The Lady of the Woods frowned, and stooped to inspect the confusion of hoofprints leading out of the book.

'Some of these hoofs were cloven,' she murmured. 'These aren't the marks of a unicorn, at any rate.' She frowned again, and stood in thought. 'Time will tell,' she said at last. And she tapped the book to make it shrink, and climbed with it back into the carriage. 'Now, home!'

The sun was setting at last. Blue shadows had crept up the tree-trunks until only their very tops still shone red; and by the deep pool below the falls, Tom the miller's son was packing up his fishing rod and tackle. He had not had a very good catch. There had been a couple of small perch earlier on, but just as the sun was sinking over the crags, just when the fish are normally keenest after the bait, a hush had fallen, an odd feeling had come over the woods, and from then on he had not had a single bite.

Tom was puzzled by it, and he definitely felt something uncanny in the air as he made his way home. He crossed the mill-stream by the narrow footbridge, and stood and listened. There was an uneasy rustling all round, not such as the wind makes, but as if there were things just out of sight, moving with some hidden purpose. Mist was gathering, and sound echoed strangely. There was a distant noise like high-pitched laughter, the nearby scamper of tiny feet, the snap of a twig behind him.

Tom moved quickly on, not looking back. He climbed the path through the trees, and soon came to the small house in its lonely clearing where he lived with his parents and grandmother.

He pushed open the door and laid his catch on the table.

'Just a couple of perch, mother. I don't know what came over the fish suddenly, just before sunset.'

'Never mind, Tom. I'll do what I can with them. Father's still down at the mill.'

'It's getting dark very quickly tonight,' said Tom, going to the fireside to take off his boots.

''Tis a change coming,' said his grandmother. Tom wondered what she meant, but she kept her old face turned towards the fire, and said no more.

That night Tom looked out of his window over the valley. The moon was up, and nearly full, and the mist was lying at the feet of the hills like sleeping ghosts. There were sounds of movement in the forest, and then there came a deep, full bellow, like a bull, but harsher, strange to Tom's ears. In another moment there came an echo. The beast bellowed again, and again the woods and rocks replied.

Tom knew there had never been an echo there before. He shouted out, 'Who's there?' and the words came back from the woods; but the voice wasn't his own, and the tone seemed different too: mocking and amused.

He said no more, closed the window on the strange world outside, and tried to go to sleep, while the whispers and bumps went on all night, inside the house and out, and the silver-blue mist crept in long folds through the Kingdom, over every field and round every house, through the cobbled streets of the town and all about the turrets of the Castle. The seeds grew, and the sleeping things stirred and stretched, and the beasts bellowed, and the Queen's Magic and Mystery came to life.

CHAPTER 2

Goblin Gold

Next day Tom was up with the sun. It was a bright, clear morning, and his only thought was that he was to help his father move a load of grain from the storehouse to the mill. He got dressed and climbed down the rickety stairway to the main room of the house, where his mother had already made the porridge. Grandmother was up from the bed where she slept in the corner, and looked more absorbed than usual, as if listening for something. At that, Tom remembered the night before, the scuttling noises and the bellowing in the woods, the creeping mist and the mocking echo that was not his own voice.

'What is it, grandmother?'

She sat down slowly at the table, and seemed unwilling to reply. 'Ah, we'll see, Tom,' she said at last.

The miller stepped in at the door; he had already been out to milk the cow, and had a troubled look on his face.

'There, father,' said his wife. 'What ails you? Eat your porridge, and don't fret.'

'I can't say what it is,' he replied, sitting down. 'But 'twas a disquieted, fidgety night, and the morn's too still to be quite as it should.'

He shook his head and started on his porridge. None of them spoke, and Tom realized how very quiet it was. The murmur of the mill-race could be heard from down the hill, but the pigeons, normally loud at this time of day, were silent in the trees. No blackbird chirped, and there was no breath of wind to stir the leaves of the poplars that stood by the house.

Suddenly they all jumped, as a furious banging shook the room. Tom looked round in alarm, to the hearth where the porridge-pot stood, the chest where their clothes were kept, the broken stool that wanted mending, and then the old oak cupboard, where preserves, cups and trenchers, and all manner of cooking things lay stored. The four of them stared at it speechless. The doors of the cupboard were nearly jumping off their hinges.

Tom moved cautiously towards it, and threw open the doors. The banging stopped. Tom peered in, and then jumped back. An ugly face was staring at him. It had small, bright eyes, a great bloated nose, a nasty scowl with crooked teeth, and over all that a tangled mass of wiry hair, with a pair of pointed ears sticking up through it. The creature was sitting in a dripping-pan and holding a ladle, which it had been using as a battering-ram on the cupboard door.

'What is it?' gasped Tom.

'What is it?' echoed the creature in a harsh, squeaky voice. 'Same to you! Do I smell porridge? I want some!' And it threw down the ladle, eased itself out of the dripping-pan, and jumped down on to the floor. Standing at its full height, it only came up to Tom's knees. It was dressed in a greenish-brownish suit and pointed-toed slippers, and had a tail out behind with a hairy tuft on the end.

Tom's mother screamed, as the creature scampered up on the table where the porridge bowls stood. Only grandmother still sat where she was. The thing gave her a wary look, and then started slurping down the porridge from the other three bowls. Just as it had its snout fairly buried, Tom's grandmother took her spoon and gave it a sharp rap on one of its pointed ears. It gave a cry of pain, and lifted its angry face, dripping with porridge.

'Get away, you nasty thing,' said grandmother, and swung her spoon again, but the creature jumped down and made for the door.

'I'll be back!' it threatened, now licking porridge from its snout, now rubbing its bruised ear. 'You'll see! I'll show you! I'm here to stay!' Then, with a final cross look and a flick of its tufted tail, the thing was gone.

The miller and his wife let out their breaths, and Tom's grandmother went on with her porridge.

'What was it, grandmother?' asked Tom.

She put down her spoon. ''Twas a goblin.'

'A goblin!' Tom exclaimed.

'And how did it get in our cupboard, I'd like to know?' asked Tom's mother, cleaning up the mess of spilt porridge.

'They come and go, do goblins. I can't say how.'

'But how do you know about goblins, grandmother?' asked Tom. 'I never knew you'd seen one.'

'Oh, I've seen 'em,' she replied. 'They swarmed pretty thick, years back. When the winter was bad they'd come, turn the milk and steal the wood. They can play many a nasty trick, can goblins, and work spells too, some of 'em.'

Tom's father looked serious. 'If that's so, we'll have to look about and be sharp. Now, Tom, are you coming with me to the mill, to check that all's well?'

They left their breakfast and set off together down the hill. The path led between old oaks, overgrown with moss, and twisting their branches this way and that. Not a leaf was stirring, but Tom thought the trees had never looked so sinister, as he hopped over their sprawling roots and dodged under the boughs that hung low overhead, and he had a nagging feeling that the path was not following its usual course. He could feel the stirring of watchful, restless things, and wasn't sorry when the mill came into sight through the trees.

At the mill they stopped to listen. There was nothing: only the mill-race. Tom's father pushed the door open, and they peered inside. There were the millstones and the great wooden cogs, all quiet in the dark.

The miller heaved a sigh of relief. 'That's all right, son. I think my eyes were playing tricks on me up at the house: it's never right to judge too quick. So if there's goblins or if there's not, let's move those sacks of grain in from the storehouse and be on with the day's work.'

So Tom went for the first sack, already beginning to forget his worries. He crossed to the storehouse, opened the door, and staggered back.

The floor, the loft, the sacks of grain and flour piled about, all were swarming with goblins. Some were shovelling grain into mouths like rabbit-holes, until their bellies puffed out and the buttons popped off their suits. Others the size of rats were tunnelling in and out of the sacks, sticking their heads out and scattering the wheat in showers. The middle of the room was a goblin dance floor. A dozen of the creatures were jigging up and down with linked arms, whisking their tails in delight, to the cracked notes of a goblin song; and, over in a corner, another goblin was pointing at the sacks of flour with a crooked stick, and with a flash of fire and smoke the sacks split and the flour shot out in heaps.

Tom stared, and then he seized up a stick and charged among them. Goblins fled squealing and cursing in all directions, the bigger ones treading on the smaller ones.

18

Flour flew up in clouds, and in no time the storehouse was empty.

Tom surveyed the devastated scene in amazement. Torn sacks were scattered across the room, and flour and grain lay mixed up everywhere, covered in confused footprints, some made by the goblins' pointed slippers, some by their bare three-toed feet. Then in the corner he saw something more worrying still. Where the goblin with the crooked stick had been making the little flashes of fire, there were heaps and heaps of something that was neither grain nor flour. Goblin magic was at work, turning their flour to sand.

'Father!' he shouted, running back to the mill. 'Come quickly!'

When Tom's father had seen the storehouse he looked more serious than ever.

''Tis a plague of them, Tom, and our livelihood going to ruin. What's to be done?'

Tom thought, and then he said, 'Grandmother. She may know something.'

'Then run, Tom. I've an idea these goblins won't stay hid for long.'

Tom ran back up the path and burst back in at the door of the cottage.

'Grandmother! How do you get rid of goblins?'

'Get rid of them, Tom?' Grandmother looked up from the material she was mending. 'You don't get rid of goblins.'

Tom threw himself down on a chair. 'There must be something you can do. How did you manage in the old days?'

'We tried, Tom. We used to trap 'em, and take their gold.'

'Gold, grandmother?'

'Aye, Tom. Every goblin has its purse of gold, and if a goblin's fairly caught, it has to hand it over. For, you see, though goblins love their gold, they love freedom more. But 'tis queer stuff, goblin gold, and not much use to humankind.'

'And did that get rid of them? You could give them their gold back, and they'd promise to go away?'

Grandmother chuckled again. 'Goblins are poor hands at keeping promises. No, there's no getting rid of a goblin, Tom.'

Tom's mother shook her head, and Tom set off back down the hill. A haze was thickening between the trees, and blurred shapes flitted through it, whispering and murmuring. But Tom gave them no heed. He was thinking hard, and by the time he got back to the mill, he had a plan.

'Tom!' his father called out. 'At last you're back! The nasty things have been leading me that much of a game of hide-and-seek, I don't know where I am! I chase them, they chase me, I carry a sack to the mill, they carry it back, and when I find it again it's turned to soot! What's to be done?'

'I've got an idea,' Tom replied. 'Just stay in the mill, and leave it to me.'

So Tom's father went into the mill and did his best to start grinding his grain, while Tom set to work. First he prised up some loose floorboards inside the storehouse, covered the hole with empty sacks, and sprinkled flour and grain on top. Then he took an old water-barrel and crawled with it under the floor of the building, which was raised up on pillars to keep the rats out. He set the barrel under the hole in the boards and lay down beside it in the dark, waiting to see what would happen.

ᴦALWAY COUNTY LIBRARIᴇ

Soon he heard pattering footsteps overhead, and the squeak of goblin voices.

'Has he gone?' hissed one.

'I think so,' rasped another.

'Time for guzzles!' shouted a third, and all the others chimed in with 'Gobbles!' 'Junkets!' 'Frolics!' 'Romps!'

In a moment, all the goblin antics had started up again. Tom could hear flour and grain being slurped down by the bushel, and the floor shook to the tread of a rowdy goblin square-dance. All of a sudden there was a squeak of amazement, the dancing stopped, and a confused mass of sacking, flour, and goblin landed in the water-barrel with a thud.

'Now I've got you!' shouted Tom. He clapped the lid on the barrel and rolled it out into the sunshine, with the goblin squealing and raging inside.

'You're my prisoner,' said Tom to the goblin, shaking the barrel, 'and I'll never let you out, unless you give me your gold.'

'Never!' shouted the goblin. 'I have magic powers! I'll be out of this barrel in less than no time!'

Now Tom thought that if the goblin really did have magic powers, it would probably be using them, and not just talking about them. So he said, 'Oh, very well, I don't mind waiting and seeing your magic. But in the meantime I'm going to keep you in a cage, and never let you go, and I won't even feed you unless you beg ever so.'

At this, the goblin burst out blubbering. 'Oh, don't do that,' it wailed. 'You can have my gold. Just let me go!'

'You'll have to give me the gold first,' said Tom, who remembered what grandmother had said about goblin promises. 'Where is it?'

'It's hidden in the big hollow tree by the river,' said

the goblin sulkily. 'Now, let me out!' But Tom had no intention of letting the goblin out just yet, and rolled the barrel all the way to the hollow oak by the side of the river.

'Now while we're having this chat, goblin, I'd like to know where you've come from. How was it that all you goblins suddenly appeared like this?'

Angry as the goblin was, it couldn't resist showing off its knowledge. 'I grew from a seed, of course! Anyone knows that. Me, I grew inside a sack of flour, with two friends. First I grew; then I saw the others start up, tiny things at first, swelling up like bread dough left to rise. And then their eyes blinked open, their arms and legs popped out and their ears uncurled, their slippers grew and their hair and tails shot out. And then the bag burst, and we were all lying in your storeroom, and fancied a bit of a dance, and then *you* came along.' The goblin fell silent, with an air of great disgust.

Tom was very thoughtful as he tipped the barrel on end and stood on it to reach up to the hollow part of the tree. 'I hope you're a truthful goblin,' he said, groping about.

'I always tell the truth!' exclaimed the goblin, sounding deeply wounded.

'Aha!' Tom drew out a clinking leather bag, and got down off the barrel. He opened it up, and, sure enough, it had in it more gold coins than he had ever thought to see in his life. Each one bore an ugly, pimply head, with the writing 'Prince of Hobgoblins, King of Pranks, and Lord of Mischief' running round the outside.

'Where did you get this from?' Tom demanded.

'It grew from a seed, of course. It's goblin gold. When are you going to let me out?'

'Very soon,' said Tom. 'Now this gold is all very well,

but what I really want is for you and your friends to stop bothering us. Now, if I were to give you your gold back, do you think you'd promise never to come near the mill or the house again?'

'Oh, *certainly* I'd promise,' gabbled the goblin delightedly. 'Word of honour—swear most solemnly— vow and declare—a goblin's word is its bond, absolutely.'

'That's what I thought,' said Tom drily. 'So I'm not going to give you your gold back.'

'What!' it shrieked. 'You doubt the word of a goblin? And one of good family and known moral uprightness!'

'I'm afraid so, yes,' went on Tom. 'This time your gold will buy your freedom. But if ever I catch you round the mill again, you won't have anything to offer me, will you? And I'll never let you go.' At this, the goblin raved and cursed in such a way that Tom felt reasonably sure that it had no more gold to offer.

'And you can tell your friends,' he continued sternly, 'that they'd better stay clear of our house and mill, because the first time I catch them they'll lose their gold, and the second time I'll put them in my big cage, and feed them only every other Thursday. And I've got lots of other traps besides the one I caught you in, so you can tell that to your friends too. Now off you go.' And he tipped the goblin out of the barrel on to the grass, in a heap of flour and sacking.

It was furious. 'Oh, I think mankind is the wickedest breed in the world!' it screeched. 'Oh, when I tell the others, they'll think the horriblest thoughts about you! Oh!' Tom rushed at it and made to stamp on its tail, but the creature was off with a bound, and vanished into the woods. Tom smiled, and clinked his bag of gold as he walked back towards the mill, where the cogs were turning and the sweet smell of fresh flour was filling the air.

All that day Tom spent trapping goblins, and by evening he had amassed a fair hoard of pimply-headed goblin coins. The miller was whistling cheerfully.

'That'll do for today, son. If they leave us in peace tonight, we'll not have done badly.'

'I think I'll stay and watch for a while,' said Tom. 'I'll follow soon.'

His father set off up the hill to the house, while Tom squatted beside one of his traps, and the shadows deepened. A sound of stirring and sighing came from the woods, but around the mill all was quiet. The goblins had learnt their lesson. Tom smiled, and set off home.

The sun was sinking behind the hills, staining the trunks of the trees an eerie red. They were like footmen in crimson livery, Tom thought, leaning over him, ushering him on down some long, dusty hall.

He hurried on, but the faster he walked, the more he imagined the trees to be coming alive. Behind him, the moon began to rise; a rustling and a creaking rose up, and the trees began to move. Their branches flexed at wrists and elbows, their bark rippled like cloth over a living body, and their knot-holes and clefts became faces that smiled. Then, all together, the trees shifted on their roots, closing over the path and opening up a new one instead. Their trunks bowed low, beckoning him on, and before Tom knew it he was running on in the new direction.

His heart began to beat fast. Now the trees were sliding this way and that, first showing him a path on one side, then closing up and offering another, where a moment before there had only been a tangle of mossy roots and ancient trunks. Tom ran and ran as if in a dream, until

24

at last he was startled by the hoot of an owl nearby. It took off, and a branch formed itself into a hand and made a snatch at it. That broke the spell. Tom made up his mind, and darted off the path.

Goblins clung chattering about the bases of the trees, and the bellowing of beasts was in Tom's ears; roots like mossy snakes slithered to stop him, and branches caught at him like bony arms; but he dodged them all and ran on, bearing always uphill. At the top of the hill he thought he could see a light: home. But whispering strands of mist were drifting to block his way, their curling fingers and empty eyes clear in the moonlight, and when he looked back he saw tree-roots groping over the rocks like fingers, ready to heave one up and throw it after him.

The next moment he was sprawling on the ground, with a root twining over him to pin him down. He tugged and pulled, while the moon stared down on him, and the mist slid in round. And then the pale light faded, the grip of the tree-root slackened, and the mist drew apart. The moon had gone behind a cloud.

Tom pulled himself free and ran full pelt for home. The trees whispered and stirred in the darkness, but nothing tried to stop him. Before long he burst into the clearing, threw open the door to the cottage, and slammed it shut behind him.

That was an evening to remember at the miller's house. The fire was banked up and the shutters were closed to keep out the sounds of the night. The four of them sat up late over a good-sized bowl of mulled cider, while Tom told them everything he had seen and heard.

'It's too much for me to fathom,' sighed the miller. 'There's been nothing like it in my time.'

There was silence, and Tom stared into the fire. 'Tell

us about the old days, grandmother. About ghosts and goblins, and the things folk used to say about them.'

'Ah, we took more heed of suchlike things then,' grandmother replied. 'There were some folk never much cared to be out of a night, for fear of seeing a ghost or a spook. Took seven years off the end of your life, so they said; but I never held with that talk. I've seen a few in my time, me that's eighty-nine now.

'And goblins, Tom. We had many a rhyme and byword for goblins, and things that come out at night. They love the night, do goblins, and a moonlit one best of all. Then they dance and howl like mad things. "Daft as a moonsick goblin", folk used to say, and to such as weren't quite right in the head we'd sing:

'Loon, loon, sing to moon;
moon, moon, laugh at loon.

'As if 'twas the moon had taken their wits, and bound them to sing to it as their master, while all it could do was laugh back at them for their pains. Some called it the eye of the night: "sun sees all by day, moon sees all by night," they used to say.'

'And what did they mean?'

'Well, their idea was there were things that best liked to be seen by the one or the other. The one lot are all that's fair and bright, dogs that guard the farm, horses, and human folk. Then there are the uncanny things, bats that flutter, and screech-owls, every one of them a dead man's soul, the old folk said. And there's nothing an owl likes so well as a bright moon, that's sure.'

'And did people think the moon really could see us?' went on Tom, deep in thoughts of the mysterious.

'The moon or the folk on the moon, either way,' answered grandmother. 'We see it, so I suppose it sees

26

us right enough. But I never paid much heed to suchlike talk.'

Tom went on staring into the fire, and thought of the goblins' spells, of the whispering ghosts in the woods, of the malice of the trees and the mocking voice in the valley that hooted back to the owls and bellowed after the beasts.

'I'll find out,' said Tom, his eyes still fixed on the fire. 'I'll find out yet what it's all about!'

CHAPTER 3

Sir Vortigern

That first day of Magic and Mystery was an eventful one at the Castle too. When Princess Eleanor woke up, she felt at once that things were wrong. And then she began to hear the sounds, a scampering and a scuffling, mixed with muffled laughs and whispers.

She threw back the curtains of her bed, and there across the room were three stumpy creatures with pointed ears and tufted tails, trying on her hats one by one and laughing at each other in the mirror.

'Out!' Eleanor shouted. She seized up a pillow and flung it among them. The goblins scattered with yelps, and Eleanor sank back in bed, feeling stunned. Then she whispered, 'Magic and Mystery. Mother, what have you *done*?' She got dressed quickly and set off for the Queen's bedchamber.

Meanwhile the Queen was waking from a deep, contented sleep. Dreams of the Lady of the Woods were fresh in her mind, and the first thing she thought of was the Wish. She sprang from bed with a smile, and was just settling herself at her dressing table when Princess Eleanor knocked on her door and came in.

'Mother! Are you all right?'

'All right? Why shouldn't I be? Really, dear! Always worrying!'

'You mean you haven't seen them yet?'

'Seen what?'

'The little men.'

The Queen's heart jumped. 'No! That sounds magical!'

'I wouldn't quite call them that,' Eleanor replied. 'I expect you'll see for yourself before long.'

And she sat herself down in a chair to keep an eye on her mother, while the Queen turned back to her dressing table. This was one of the parts of the day the Queen enjoyed most. With a delicate yawn, she pulled open a drawer and reached for her comb. Then she snatched her hand away with a cry. Something had yawned back.

'It's the comb,' Eleanor announced, peering over her mother's shoulder. 'It's come to life.'

It had. The comb was sitting up now, its silver teeth bristling, and a small, distinct voice cried out, 'Hands off!'

'Oh!' purred the Queen. 'How *charming*!'

But Eleanor was less sure. 'I wouldn't touch it if I were you. It doesn't look very friendly.'

The Queen was not listening. 'It's started!' she moaned ecstatically. 'Oh, it's started!'

The comb stared back. 'I'm delighted to hear it,' it replied. 'Perhaps now you'll close the drawer so I can get back to sleep.'

'Oh, not yet,' wheedled the Queen. 'Wouldn't you like to comb my hair?'

'No! It tickles, and the hair gets in my teeth. And besides, I'm sleepy.' And it crept to the back of the drawer, muttering.

'Well!' said the Queen, and shut the drawer. 'There's still my hairbrush. And this time let's try not to upset it.'

In the next drawer they found the Queen's hairbrush, curled up like a sleeping hedgehog. Beside it stood a cluster of make-up pots, snoring so that their lids lifted and settled again noisily. The curling tongs were stretching and scratching themselves with their handles, while the nail-file scraped itself idly against the velvet lining of the drawer.

The Queen peered into the drawer, entranced. 'Now then,' she said sweetly. 'Rise and shine!'

The make-up pots yawned in turn so that their lids rattled; the hairbrush uncurled lazily, and the nail-file started with a guilty look.

'Quite right,' went on the Queen. 'You mustn't scratch the furniture, you know! Really! Pets are such a responsibility.'

Now the hairbrush blinked awake. 'Your Majesty,' it purred, sitting up on its four paws, with its bristles uppermost. 'I've been asleep such a very, very, very long time! And last night I heard the loudest trumpet, and since then I've been waking up ever so, ever so slowly'—here it yawned again—'and now I think I'd like to brush your hair, if you didn't mind.'

'It would be a real pleasure,' said the Queen, and the brush scampered up her arm and on to her shoulder, and then bounded into her hair, where it dived and pulled and surfaced again, with coos of delight. Eleanor watched apprehensively, and then she heard a further chorus of yawns, one from the full-length mirror that stood across the room, another from the marquetry chest.

'Good morning, Your Majesty!' said the mirror, dropping a deep curtsy. 'How very well you're looking today!' And then it sucked its breath in loudly and bent itself inwards, giving the Queen a dainty, wasp-like waist.

'That's very kind of you,' laughed the Queen. 'But I think I'd rather see what I really look like.'

'Oh, *fatter* than that?' retorted the mirror, and puffed

itself out so that the Queen's reflection swelled like a balloon.

'No,' she said, rather vexed, and then to the hairbrush, 'Ow! You're pulling too hard!' But the hairbrush was deaf to the world, and could only plunge and cavort in the Queen's flowing hair, while the mirror pulled itself in and blew itself out, making the Queen look like a humpback, a spindly giant, a dwarf, and then a long-armed ape.

Eleanor was beginning to get angry. 'I'd teach that mirror a lesson if I were you. Here, let me try and get that brush out of your hair.'

'Don't you touch my mirror. It's all in fun, and besides, it's seven years bad luck. But this brush—it is a little—ow—a little tiresome.' She turned her back on the pulsating monstrosity in the mirror, and began struggling with her hair, which only made the brush burrow in deeper.

'Never mind,' she sighed. 'Maybe it'll go to sleep again. How about some make-up?'

She peered into the drawer and reached for the rouge pot, which stepped forward proudly, lifting its lid with a tiny hand.

'A very wise choice, ma'am,' said the pot. 'I promise satisfaction!'

'Huh!' said one of the other pots. 'If the Queen wants to look like a flamingo, I'm sure she'll be very satisfied indeed!'

'Yes,' sniffed another. 'Personally, I think a pale complexion's handsomest. Allow me to offer my services. A nice touch of powder?'

'A very low taste,' sneered another pot. 'We don't want her to look as if she's seen a ghost, do we? No, I agree with my friend Rouge: there's nothing like the rosy glow of health. But he's so half-hearted about it! Choose me instead. Your Majesty, choose Vermilion!' And the pot lifted its lid and bowed low.

The Queen was hesitating, not wanting to make enemies, when a confused cry rose up from the next drawer. Trembling rather, she pulled it open, and saw all her perfumes, scents, and essences jumping up and down and waving their stoppers in their hands.

'What's sight compared to smell?' demanded one. 'Don't bother with them: use us!'

'Rosewater!'

'Cologne!'

'Oil of lavender!'

'Me!'

'No, me!'

Meanwhile, the rouge pot had crept up behind the proud vermilion and given it a sharp kick.

'That was the lowest, dirtiest, trickiest—' began the vermilion, picking itself up, while bright red powder lay scattered over the drawer, and the white powder pots were screaming in anguish.

'Oh, my beautiful colour! I'll be pink for life!'

The clamour was rising. The curling tongs were having an argument with the sleepy comb, and the mirror was posturing in front of the old marquetry chest, which was spluttering out in a deep voice, 'Have a care! I would have you know, madam, that I am a self-respecting chest! I warn you—'

The Queen slammed all her drawers shut, carefully disentangled the hairbrush, and set it down on the table-top, where it began creeping about on all fours.

'Well, that'll just have to do. Make-up's so bad for the complexion, anyway. Now then! Little men, you said? I think it's high time we were going down to breakfast, and then we'll see what we shall see!'

Patting her hair down, the Queen breezed out into the corridor, and Princess Eleanor followed. The Queen's three ladies were waiting for them, looking pale and flustered, and then Lady Linda jumped aside with a scream, as a torrent of small bodies swept past. Eleanor caught only a glimpse of wiry-haired heads, pointed slippers pounding on the floorboards, and the lash of tufted tails, and heard a confused cry of, 'It's breakfast time! Breakfast time! Frolics! Gambols! Junkets!'

'Ooh!' crowed the Queen. 'Come on!' And she hurried after them to the royal breakfast parlour. It was a snug room, overlooking a small courtyard with a herb garden in it; but today it was anything but peaceful. The King sat alone at the head of the table, attempting to eat his breakfast, while one goblin shook the table-leg so that the crockery rattled, another fished out piping hot sausages from the dish, and threw them to a third and the third to a fourth, and a fifth stood on the sideboard declaiming goblin poetry, to the delight of no one at all.

The King jabbed a goblin in the paw with a fork, and rang the bell furiously. Horrified footmen appeared, who began chasing the goblins vainly around the room. And all the time the Queen still stood in the doorway, her hands clasped in wonder.

'What *charming* creatures!' she burst out at last. '*Such* an enchanting idea! I'd love one for a pet!'

The goblins, however, looked anything but tame. As the footmen chased them out through the door, the last one turned to gibber out curses and shake its fist, and then it was gone.

'"Charming", my dear?' queried the King, as the Queen sat down at the table. '"Enchanting"? What *can* you mean! I believe the Castle's under a curse! Why, I was told we could have no eggs this morning, because they had all been turned into lumps of coal; luckily, the coal had also been turned into eggs, so that was all right. But the Head Cook says the creatures are running riot in the kitchens, while the Lord Chamberlain informs me that he had to stop the Crown Jewels from walking off with themselves. What can be the meaning of it?'

The Queen looked uncomfortable, as she cautiously examined a boiled egg. 'I admit that it's not *quite* what I was expecting . . . '

'Not quite what you were expecting!' echoed the King. 'What *do* you mean, my dear?'

'Oh, it's the ring, Michael, the ring with the wish, from the Lady of the Woods.' She looked at her husband appealingly, while the other four at the table, who knew about the wish, watched with apprehension.

'Ah. So you made your wish?'

The Queen nodded.

'And might one enquire what it was you wished for?'

'Magic and Mystery,' replied the Queen, rather nervously.

'Magic,' repeated the King, 'and Mystery. Not goblins? Or witchcraft? Not disorder and commotion? You're sure none of those words slipped out by mistake at the same time?'

'No, Michael. I quite clearly wished for Magic and Mystery, and nothing else. The Lady of the Woods said I should wish for something I couldn't get any other way, and so I have. And I'm sure it's all right: her magic can only really be good magic, can't it?'

'I hope you're right. But really, my dear, I don't know what made you do it.'

'It was obvious, Michael. It was the only thing I didn't have.'

'Well, you've got it now,' grumbled the King, 'and so have the rest of us.'

Just then the doors opened again, and a page came in and bowed. 'A troop of knights, your Majesties—just arrived in the courtyard, and craving an audience. Shall I tell them to wait?'

'Knights!' beamed the Queen. 'More magic and mystery, I know it! Tell them to come to the Throne Room. Come on, everyone!'

The Queen hurried off, and Eleanor slipped away down the gallery to a window overlooking the main courtyard. There they were, just as the page had said: seven knights, and they looked rather a motley crowd. One of them seemed unable to keep awake, and slouched so far down in the saddle that he was nearly falling off; another one had a shield which looked as if it was covered in millions of tiny dots, while another was all covered in bags and bundles like a tinker.

A trumpet fanfare sounded in welcome, and the knights almost stampeded. Then the Chamberlain came towards them down the steps and welcomed them to the Castle.

'Your speech is the summit of courtesy,' declared one of the knights. 'You do us infinite honour, as I shall not scruple to enumerate.'

'No time for all that,' put in another. 'Are we going in or not?'

'I think I may just stay here,' remarked the sleepy one with a yawn. 'It's too much effort altogether.'

The knight with the dots frowned at them and dismounted.

'Sir Vortigern, at your service. My ancestors would be disgraced if I did not accept your invitation with alacrity, my good sir. Never mind the others: they'll follow, probably.' So saying, he led the astonished Lord Chamberlain by the arm inside the Castle. There was a general clanking of dismounting knights, and Eleanor hurried into the Throne Room to take her place before they arrived.

'Sir Vortigern,' read out the Chamberlain from the slip of paper he had been handed. 'Son of Cadwal, son of Morind, son of Albanack, son of Bladud, son of Helic, son of Gorboman, son of Cassiblane, son of Meredoc, son of—'

'Aren't we going to find out anything about the others?' whispered the Queen.

'At least we'll know plenty about this one,' remarked Princess Eleanor drily.

'Hm,' murmured the King. 'We hate to cut short your worthy genealogy, but perhaps we might learn the names of these other gentlemen?'

'By all means, sire,' said Sir Vortigern with a sigh. 'This is Sir Politesse, a most courteous knight.'

'Indeed,' said Sir Politesse, advancing with the most exquisite bow ever seen, 'you do me too much honour. Your Majesties, I beg you to consider me your most humble, loyal, and devoted servant. Grant this boon, and Sir Politesse is content.'

The next one pushed forward.

'Sir Dizziwind, Your Majesty,' explained Sir Vortigern. 'A valiant knight. Hasty, perhaps; impetuous, even—'

'That's enough talk, Vortigern. Mustn't waste the King's time. Or ours, for that matter. So let's just keep it all brief.' And he stood impatiently tapping his foot while the next knight stepped up.

'Sir Palindrome, Your Majesties. A most easy-going knight. Actually,' he added in a whisper, 'he never can make his mind up about anything.'

Sir Palindrome advanced, with his shield on his arm. It bore a two-headed horse on a green field, each head pointing a different way and each smiling, and the motto 'I'm happy either way'. While he was deciding who he should bow to first, the King or the Queen, another knight pushed forward.

'Sir Bivouac here, bluff, no nonsense, that's me. The outdoor life's the best. Fresh air, a clean pitch for the tent, that's what counts. Nice to meet you, Your Majesties.'

That only left one, who now staggered forward under the weight of a huge rucksack. Pots and pans dangled at his elbows, while spare blades for his sword, extra hay for his horse, and gourds of water hung all up his sides and down his legs.

'Sir Reticule, Your Majesty,' explained Sir Vortigern. 'He's what you might call our baggage train.'

'He looks as if he's carrying everything but the kitchen sink,' whispered Princess Eleanor to her mother.

'Your pardon, Highness,' put in Sir Reticule in reply. 'As it was somewhat heavy, I left it strapped to my horse.'

'And that only leaves Sir Slugabed,' said Sir Vortigern. 'But where is he? There are only six of us here!'

'He said he didn't like to get off his horse once he was on it,' explained Sir Dizziwind. 'And, frankly, I think he's got a point. Never any sense wasting time. Why not be off? Day's half gone. There's dragons to slay!'

'Sir Dizziwind speaks well,' said Sir Vortigern, turning to the King. 'Our knightly duty calls. Were there more time, I could tell you many tales of the glorious deeds of my ancestors, all three thousand nine hundred and seventy-two of them—every one of whose coats of arms is shown on my shield. A special microscope had to be made for the armourer who painted it.'

Sir Dizziwind was heaving sigh after sigh and tapping his foot, while Sir Bivouac was already drawing in deep breaths, longing for the fresh air of the woods and hills.

'But, as I say, duty calls. Your Majesties' kingdom is aswarm with manticores, beset with beasts, and groaning with griffins . . . So, with Your Majesties' permission . . . '

The King frowned. 'Manticores? Beasts?'

'Indeed, sire. All night we rode hard after them. Then at dawn we lost the scent rather . . . But never fear! The plague of monsters that has fallen on your realm will soon be over. To horse!'

Sir Reticule shifted the weight of his rucksack, Sir Politesse began to doff and curtsy, and the whole procession backed untidily out into the courtyard. At the last moment Sir Palindrome decided to go with them, and hurried to catch up. Before long, the sound of hoofs was heard from outside, and the seven knights were off for the wilds, after monsters and glory.

The Princess watched them go with a kind of amused disbelief; she couldn't say whether she thought the knights were funny, or just horrible. The Queen, however, heaved a wistful sigh. 'What chivalry! So romantic! They look just as if they'd ridden out of a storybook!' And this, of course, was a very perceptive comment.

The King looked less pleased. 'Manticores,' he murmured. 'Dragons, griffins . . . Things look serious, my dear. I shall have to summon the Council. I believe the kingdom is in danger.'

CHAPTER 4

The King's Council

All next morning the King's Council debated. Grave murmurings could be heard from the Throne Room, and worried messengers kept arriving from different parts of the kingdom with new reports. Princess Eleanor walked past the door quite a few times, wondering what was going on inside.

Another puzzle had to do with her mother. She hadn't appeared for breakfast, and the last time Eleanor had seen her was last night, when she had tottered to bed after dinner looking rather pale. First there had been the haunted pastries, then the fight between the candlesticks, and then the jester, whose magic tricks had for once really worked, with the result that Lady Clara had been turned into a duck. Perhaps, Eleanor thought, perhaps after all that she's finally had enough.

Around lunchtime the doors to the Throne Room opened, and Eleanor watched as the King and his counsellors trooped out, grim-faced. Suddenly the Queen appeared, dressed in her riding habit, and looking as bright as ever.

'What's this, my dear?' said the King. 'Are you going out?'

'Yes, Michael,' replied the Queen mysteriously. 'I'm going riding.'

'At a time like this?'

'What time could be better?'

'But there are the most disturbing reports—hauntings, goblins, even creatures so strange that the Court Librarian can find them in none of his books. I have all the complaints of our subjects right here,'—and he waved a thick bundle of papers—'and they make grim and bizarre reading, I can tell you.'

'Ooh,' purred the Queen, fixing the bundle with greedy eyes.

'Please, mother,' begged Eleanor, coming forward. 'Haven't you had enough? What about last night?'

'Ah, poor Lady Clara!' sighed the Queen. 'They say the jester has already filled a large notebook with useless spells, and the Court Physician has had to treat him for duck bites. And Lady Clara is normally so very gentle and considerate! Still, one might say she has had unusual provocation.'

'I don't think you realize how serious this is,' insisted the King. 'Why, any child might cast a spell on his playfellows without meaning to. And the goblins can work enchantments, too.'

'But the Lady of the Woods, you know, Michael. Her magic can only really be good in the end, can't it? And, Michael, dear, won't you let me borrow your bundle of papers to look at, so I can see?'

'Very well,' said the King. 'We'll see if that changes your tune.'

The Queen grabbed hold of the bundle in delight, and sailed off back to her chamber, with Eleanor following suspiciously. When the Queen burst into her room Lady Linda and Lady Samantha were waiting for her.

'I've got it!' shouted the Queen. 'The catalogue of attractions! Oh, what shall we see first? Apple orchard whose trees bear nothing but bars of soap . . . haunted inn—ghost like a mirror, turns itself into any shape it chooses . . . echo with a voice of its own . . . bogeyman sprang out at a coach: its tongue was a yard long, and its eyes were on stalks . . . Oh, I don't know where to begin!'

'Oh, mother,' Eleanor protested. 'You don't want to see a bogeyman, do you!'

'See everything, do everything. That's my motto. Look: will o' the wisps lead travellers astray. Now that would be exciting, only you have to get lost to enjoy it properly . . .'

'But dragons, your Majesty,' ventured Lady Samantha. 'And griffins! Aren't they . . . fierce?'

'Really!' the Queen complained. 'What a lot of chickens! You're not afraid, are you?'

'I don't mind seeing the soap-trees,' said Lady Linda, 'but I refuse absolutely to see any bogeymen.'

'But you'll have to if one jumps out at you,' replied the Queen brightly. 'Oh, what a *pity* Lady Clara is indisposed! Come on, you lot. Get changed, so we can set off.'

Princess Eleanor sighed and went to get changed, determined to do her best to keep her mother out of trouble.

At first things did not go too badly. Everyone liked the soap-orchard. The four of them wandered about among the trees gazing up at the young, swelling soap-bars in their nests of apple leaves: orange sandalwood, tangy lemon, or black coal-tar; and the air was heavy with their scent.

'Quaint,' murmured the Queen. 'Quite quaint.'

She broke off a small bar of lemon soap, the writing just puffing out so you could read it, and tucked it in her girdle. Then with a sigh of delight she led the others back to their horses, and the party continued on its way.

It was after that things got worse. They had been

41

heading west, and now they had come to the edge of the woods. The sun shone more faintly here; a whispering haze hung between the trees, and the air felt chill.

And then they heard the squealing. High above the ground, a pig struggled and kicked, wrapped firmly round in mossy boughs that looked as if they had taken centuries to grow. The four of them gazed at it, and even the Queen shuddered.

'Eerie!' she whispered. 'Imagine when the tree stooped down and picked it up!'

'That's too much,' stated Lady Linda.

'Can't we go back?' pleaded Lady Samantha.

'Please, mother,' Princess Eleanor added.

'Don't be silly,' the Queen replied, pulling herself together. 'We haven't seen the haunted inn yet. Come on!'

Dutifully the others followed her along the misty edge of the forest, until they came to the very last village before the trees finally closed in and the deep woods began. In this village, down by the riverside, stood the Eagle Inn. The party rode up to the door, where the Queen dismounted eagerly, and got out her list.

'Ah, Master Richard!' began the Queen, who knew the innkeeper well. 'We are here in search of Magic and Mystery. Now then, we understand you have a most unusual ghost; also that your inn is swarming with goblins, but I think perhaps we've seen enough of those already.' (At this her ladies-in-waiting nodded firmly.) 'And it says here that you are host to our gallant friends, Sir Vortigern and his associates, whom we would naturally wish to see, and question on the subject of manticores and dragons. Well?'

Master Richard looked rather unhappy. He had hoped

the Queen might have come in answer to the complaint he had sent to the King, begging for something to be done about the plague of enchantments that had fallen on his inn.

'All you say is true,' he admitted. 'The knights are out questing, though, all except Sir Slugabed, that is. But we've still got our goblins. I was a seafarer many a year before I took to innkeeping, and in some ports they swarmed like rats; but I've never known 'em as bad as now. And then, of course, there's the ghost . . . '

'Oh, the ghost!' exclaimed the Queen. 'And it turns itself into people and gives them a nasty shock! Isn't that right?'

'A nasty shock is about right. Even the goblins don't like it, and that's saying something, if you take my meaning.'

'Are you sure you really want a nasty shock, mother?' cautioned Princess Eleanor. 'You may say this magic is only ever good, but it can still be bad for the nerves.'

'Nonsense,' retorted the Queen. 'I haven't seen a ghost yet, and I mean to. It's all part of the fun. Now then,' she went on, turning to Lady Linda, who had been standing by her side. Her voice broke off, and she stared in horror at the exact likeness of herself which stood far too close to her, holding the bridle of a horse exactly like hers. The vision smiled straight into her eyes, then looked down and took from its girdle a small bar of lemon soap, with a few apple-leaves attached. The Queen let out a cry, and clutched at her side, where her own bar of soap still hung. She looked up again, and the vision smiled, fading mockingly into mist, until there was nothing between herself and Lady Linda but empty air.

After that, it was some time before the party could go

on. The Queen had to be helped into the inn, uttering small, shuddering cries. Princess Eleanor chased off the goblins, giving one of them a cruel pinch on the snout with the fire-tongs, and Master Richard hurried off for spiced wine and cakes.

The Queen seemed more herself after eating, but she did not mention the subject of ghosts again. 'Well,' she said weakly, 'shall we carry on?'

Eleanor was staggered. 'You can't mean it, mother! Not after the shock you've had!'

'But I want to see the knights,' complained the Queen. 'Which way did they go, anyway?'

'North,' replied Master Richard. 'I don't suppose they've got far. Well, they were hard at it until quite late, drinking to their heroic deeds and all.'

'Boys will be boys!' exclaimed the Queen cheerfully. 'Come on, you lot! We'll catch them up, and then we'll see some fun: and no nasty shocks!'

Princess Eleanor heaved a sigh and followed her mother out of the inn. Very soon all four were riding north along the edge of the forest. The afternoon was passing. Wisps of haze obscured the sun, and the wind made a restless stirring among the trees. Eleanor felt a sense of foreboding growing on her. She wished her mother would decide she had had enough, and head for home.

Just then, they heard the sound of hoofs galloping along the track behind them, and a knight charged by, his lance levelled. He pulled to a halt and lifted his visor. It was Sir Vortigern, as they saw at once by the myriad coloured dots on his shield and banner.

'Your Majesty!' he let out in surprise. 'Pardon my haste, ma'am: have you seen a Beast come lolloping by? No matter—I hear its cry. Ladies, my compliments!'

And with that, his visor was down and his lance lowered, and he was off, while a faint baying resounded from deep inside the woods.

'A beast!' breathed the Queen in excitement. 'This is *really* something new!' And without waiting for the others, she dug her heels into her horse's sides and galloped after Sir Vortigern.

'Come back!' shouted Princess Eleanor. And, without pausing for thought, she too spurred her horse, and plunged into the forest.

CHAPTER 5

A Toadstool Dance

Princess Eleanor rode her fastest, dodging trees and ducking under branches. Ahead she caught a last glimpse of the Queen, before she passed over a rise between beech trees and was gone. By the time Eleanor found her way to the spot, there was no sign of her mother at all. A light breeze had sprung up, making all the woods echo with gentle crackles and whispers, any one of which might have been the sound of a horse and rider a long way off. She looked over her shoulder. She could still find the way back, she thought: best to climb the next hill, and hope for some sight of her mother.

So Eleanor rode down the other side of the hillock, forded a shallow stream and began to climb the rocky slope beyond. She was in the true ancient forest now. Moss-grown oaks towered above her, and among their coiling roots strange toadstools sprouted waist-high. Some were like delicate clumps of bells, each ready to chime out its own note if shaken by the wind; others had lacy veils draped from their caps, as if meant for some goblin bride; others were squat, one-legged stools, made for goblins to sit upon and brood.

She was so taken up with the strange sights of the wood that she was quite surprised to come across a path. She decided to follow it, and soon came to the top of the hill. Here the trees thinned, and below lay the river, whispering up to her through the haze.

In the middle of the scene there stood a mill, its wheel endlessly turning, adding its trundle and splash to the

46

murmur of the river and the woods. The whole picture looked as if it were sunk in an enchanted sleep, with nothing moving or changing, only the wheel turning on and on forever.

Princess Eleanor trotted forward down the hill. Just as she came to the door of the mill, a figure stepped out, ghostly white from head to toe. Eleanor started back with a cry, and then another joined it, this time dressed in a more ordinary brown.

'Don't be alarmed,' the second figure said. 'That's only father: he's no ghost that I know of.'

'Bless you, no,' laughed the miller. 'This is only honest flour, which is a kind of clothing I wear pretty often, belonging as it does to my trade.'

'Oh!' said the Princess, recovering herself. 'I do beg your pardon! It's just that I've seen one ghost already today, and I'm looking for my mother. She's lost in the woods!'

'That could be bad,' said Tom, for that was who it was. 'And after dark it could be very bad. I think I'd better help you find her.'

'Would you? I'm very worried about her. She's just so madly keen on seeing sights, you see. First this, then that: she insisted on seeing a ghost, and it gave her the fright of her life. And now she's gone galloping into the woods after a questing knight . . . and a beast.'

'Don't worry,' said Tom. 'Show me where you saw her last, and we'll see what we can do. It'll be easier if you leave your horse here.'

Eleanor dismounted.

'Won't the goblins do something to it?'

'Oh, I don't think so,' smiled Tom. 'We have an understanding here with the goblins. They stay in the woods and don't bother us, and in return we leave them alone, for which they're very grateful.'

'That sounds rather back to front.'

'I'll tell you how it works,' replied Tom, tethering her horse. 'I trap them, you see,' he went on, as they set off together through the woods. 'And I've learnt some funny things that way, too.'

'You mean you've *talked* to them? What was it like? What did they say?'

'They're queer things, goblins. For one thing, there's lots of different sorts. Some are always dancing, and others can cast spells. There are some that keep talking in rhyme, and another sort are all stiff and bookish, and use nothing but long words: the other goblins call them bookworms. I could tell you of some strange things I've seen in these woods, and I daresay we'll see a few of them as we go.'

They had come to the hillock with the beech trees on top, and Tom stood for a moment, listening. Then he led them off again, back towards the river. Soon he motioned to Eleanor to move silently.

'There's a place up ahead where the deer come down to drink,' he whispered. 'That beast may be there, and perhaps the knight and your mother along with it. But we don't know what manner of a beast it is: it may be fierce at bay, or there may be nothing. But we'll go quietly, in case of danger.'

The pair crept slowly on, pushing the springy arms of the bushes aside with as little noise as possible. Before long the trees came to an end. Before them was a stretch of bare rock, with the river winding over it in sunken channels. And there, drinking from a rocky pool, they saw the beast.

It was as tall as a good-sized horse, but to look at was more like a goat. Its white coat was flecked with golden spots, and it had a pair of long, curving horns in addition to tusks like those of a boar. As they watched, it lifted its head and looked straight at them. From its chin hung a blue beard of hair, and its two mournful eyes shone and stared like a pair of full moons. Then it gave a bit of a snort and lowered its head, and the great twisted horns began to turn this way and that. For a moment it looked threatening, but then it turned and cantered off along the rocky shelf and into the wood.

Tom and the Princess, who had been crouching closer in to the trees, breathed a joint sigh of relief.

'Have you ever seen a creature like that before?' whispered the Princess.

'Not just like that, no, though I've seen many a strange thing besides. Now if that was your mother's beast, it would seem that the valiant knight has lost its trail, and we're no better off. But there's a clearing not far away, where we might have better luck.'

Tom led the way through thick undergrowth along a faint animal track, until they came to the edge of a glade. There was an old stump in the middle of it, and an unearthly collection of toadstools of every form and colour imaginable; but there was no sign of a knight or of the Queen. They exchanged disappointed glances, and then Tom took a harder look across the clearing, and put his finger to his lips.

'Do you want to see how goblins behave when they think there's no one watching them?' he whispered.

'Yes,' the Princess whispered back, wondering what he meant; but as she watched, the stump began to move. It had a floppy, brownish toadstool growing on top of it, and a short twig sticking up on either side just beneath, while a pair of small cobwebs hung across the front, sprinkled with dewdrops. This, at least, was Eleanor's first impression. She blinked, and now she saw that the toadstool was actually a floppy hat, that the twigs were ears, the sparkling cobwebs were really a pair of spectacles, and the whole wrinkled surface of the stump was a goblin's drab-coloured suit and folded arms and legs.

She let out a gasp, and Tom motioned her to keep silent. 'It's a bookworm,' he whispered. 'See: it's got a book with it.'

It was true. As the goblin sat itself up and began to pace the clearing with one hand behind its back, she saw that in its other it held a small leather-bound volume.

'The author's pericranium must be perfectly periphrastic,' it was saying, in a tone of polite scorn. 'His ulterior lucubrations can scarcely mitigate the adumbrated persiflage of the proem. Not a scintill of sense to be seen; a gamut of giddy galvanic gabbledy-hooha to make scholarship scream and wisdom wobble.' It sniffed and shook its head, and paced out of the clearing, looking again like a walking stump as it faded into the shadows.

'What did all that mean?' whispered Eleanor.

'Who knows?' replied Tom. 'But look there!' He pointed with his finger to something neither of them had seen at first. Across the clearing there was a goblin playing on a swing that hung from the branch of a tree, dizzily swooping up and down and back, with a delighted grin on its face. As they watched, the sound of voices reached their ears from nearby. At once, the swinging goblin hopped down, its grin gone, and ran off into the wood, and the swing, which turned out to be another goblin with very long arms, dropped from the branch and loped after it.

Eleanor hoped at first that the new voices might be human, but she was soon convinced by their shrill and squeaky accents that here was a pair of goblins ambling up, deep in talk.

'They're rhymesters,' whispered Tom. 'If we listen we might learn something.'

'She's ridden deep, Dactyl,' they heard one say. 'She's in the net.'

'And, Spondee, when the moon looks down, things will happen and things will change.'

'When the mist's in, and the moon's up . . . I feel only half a goblin, when there's no moon to look down on us.'

Then the goblin called Dactyl drew his friend by the arm, and the pair seated themselves on a large toadstool.

'Ah, the moon's our master all right,' Dactyl whispered. 'But a hard one. Haven't you heard what the bookworms say? That the Eye of the Night is the eye of an Enchanter—the Bold Enchanter of the Moon.'

Both goblins looked nervously around. 'The moon . . . the Eye of the Night . . . the Bold Enchanter's Ghostly Eye . . . What is it really, Dactyl, this thing that scans us from the sky?'

'The moon, Spondee . . . they say the moon's a mighty mass of cheese: of Cheddar cliffs and Edam Plains, of creamy brooks and milky seas; and there, beside the Yoghurt Fen, there dwells a race of Moonish Men.'

'Mild and milky, Moonmen of the marshes . . . '

The other goblin nodded. 'But high above the Edam Plain live another sort: the wild and wicked Hillmen; and the Bold Enchanter is wickedest of them all. And wretched woe his evil mind has brought to guiltless Goblinkind!'

'Tell me, then,' urged Spondee in his squeaky goblin voice. 'Tell me what the Enchanter's like.'

Dactyl leant close, and whispered so that Tom and Eleanor could hardly hear.

'The Enchanter's tall and dark and grim, and lives by malice, greed, and sin. A fondue moat ten fathoms deep and sentinels who never sleep protect the Enchanter in his den, while he weaves spells to conjure men . . . Stars and comets are his slaves; he holds the power to open graves, to marshal ghosts in misty ranks, and send them out upon his pranks . . . he has a thorny magic staff, a midget with a wicked laugh, a warty toad with venomous breath, a portrait autographed by Death, and twenty other magic things, like jars that talk and chairs with wings . . . I pray that I may never fall into that Bold Enchanter's thrall!'

The goblin drew back with a shiver. The whispering mist drew round them, and the forest seemed to stir with expectation, already longing for the night, when it would once more come alive under the eye of the moon.

'But come, I've told you quite enough of all this moony cheesy stuff. Let's leave such spooky thoughts for now, and start a proper goblin row.'

The goblin let out a shrill shriek and leapt to the ground, and countless others sprang from behind every toadstool. The next moment, the two rhymesters were swept up in a tide of prancing goblin bodies and whisking tails. One of them set up a cry of 'A Toadstool Dance! A Toadstool Dance!' It vaulted over the nearest toadstool, which sprang back into place as if made of rubber; the rest took up the shout, and soon they were all playing a wild game of follow-my-leader, singing and shrieking and stamping out the time, while their chief took them bounding over this toadstool and that, through a thicket of slender stems standing like the strings of a harp, swinging round another shaped like a starburst or a merry-go-round, climbing the greasy top of a mushroom like a maypole, and dancing beneath a great frilled fungus that sheltered them like a bandstand.

Then they began vaulting over each other, and hurling one another aside by the tufts of their tails in their wild eagerness to catch up with the leader, always a toadstool ahead. The dance grew wilder and wilder, and Tom and the Princess stole back from the edge of the clearing.

'Do you think all that was true, what the goblin said about the moon, and the Bold Enchanter?' whispered Princess Eleanor, as they walked together back to the mill.

'I can't say. They're fond of lies, are goblins, but they know some things we don't, that's sure. And it seems likely enough that the moon's master of all this magic, and looks down at night to see that things are all as it wishes.'

Eleanor opened her mouth, and then thought better of it. She would have liked to tell Tom about the ring and the Wish, but she didn't like to admit that the enchantments were all the fault of her mother. But what *was* happening, really? She looked at Tom.

'You've thought a lot about all this, haven't you? Do you mind if I come back again—if there's anything I want to discuss?'

'Whenever you like,' said Tom. 'And here: something to remind you of your day in the woods.' He reached into his pocket and handed her one of the pimply-headed goblin coins.

Eleanor took it with a smile, and got on her horse, while Tom gazed curiously at the rich bridle and trappings.

'I hope your mother comes home safe—my lady.'

'I'll go back to the inn now and see. Probably she'll have turned up there—one of the knights will have found her.'

Tom nodded. 'And don't worry too much about what a pack of goblins says. She'll be all right.'

Eleanor turned her horse along the path where Tom pointed, trying not to worry. But evening was drawing in. The shadows were gathering, and a restless murmur ran through the woods.

At the inn, her worries increased. Neither the Queen nor any of the knights had been seen. Lady Linda and Lady Samantha, however, had ridden straight back to the Castle and raised the alarm, and a party of the King's guard had just arrived. Aided by some of the villagers who knew the paths, they were preparing to split up and search the forest by torchlight.

Eleanor settled herself in a corner of the main room of the inn, determined to sit up until the Queen was found. There, wrapped in her cloak, she worried by turns about magic, the moon, and her mother, the goblins, lakes of milk and mountains of cheese, and the Bold Enchanter himself . . . and so she drifted into dreams.

CHAPTER 6

The Proclamation

Eleanor was dreaming of the moon. She seemed to look out over the smooth, creamy plains where the Moonmen had their towns, with the Enchanter's Castle beyond, reared up against a dark sky on its jagged crust of Cheddar cheese.

While she dreamt, the sunset faded and the moon rose. Deep in the woods, a dark, bat-like Thing blinked awake, stretched, and unfolded its wings. It dropped from the branch where it slept out of sight in the day, and flapped slowly off, down out of the woods, dark against the whispering, moonlit mist. At the first village it flew in through the window of an inn, and settled unseen over the chair of Princess Eleanor. It was a Nightmare.

The Princess had been dreaming she was one of the wild and wicked Moonmen of the Mountains, returning from a raid with a great load of Stilton, stolen from the peaceable lowlanders. She was joking with her companions, one of whom was the miller's son, as they passed over the drawbridge into the Enchanter's Castle. Savoury steam came bubbling up from the fondue moat below, and cheesy sentinels bowed low as the cavalcade passed inside the gates.

And then, just as the dark creature settled over her chair, a change came. The portcullis fell with a rattle, and she was trapped. Ghosts shrieked from their graves, trumpets blared, and goblins swarmed from every doorway, strapping on armour and helmets and seizing up their swords. Now she was running down endless corridors, turning again and again, with always the sickly smell of hot cheese stifling her, and goblin feet flapping behind in pursuit. She tried to shout, but no voice would come, and when she turned a corner there was the Bold Enchanter, tall and grim, with his winged chair and books of spells, and the chase was over.

But then the vision lost its power. Outside the moon had passed behind a cloud; the Nightmare's smile faded, and it flapped off back towards the woods. At the same moment Princess Eleanor realized she was awake.

The moon, she thought: magic, goblins, the woods . . . her mother. She looked round, slowly remembering where she was. It was late. There was a roaring fire in the grate, and a mass of candles blazed from a large table in the middle of the room. Four of the knights were sitting at it, eating noisily. Ale tankards went up and down between mouths and table, and pieces of cold chicken were being passed from hand to hand. The only break in the feasting came for jokes and roars of laughter, during which either the ale or the candles got knocked over. Just then Master Richard appeared.

'Hey, innkeeper, hey! More ale here!'

'More chicken, Master Richard!'

'And more candles too, Master Seafarer: can't see what we're doing!'

'More grog for the hands, Master Mariner! Scurvy ship, this!'

The knights produced a blast of laughter, and then fell again to stuffing themselves. Two of them had their backs turned to the Princess, but she knew them from their surcoats: the one in green, dotted with little white tents, must be Sir Bivouac, and the other was Sir Dizziwind, his blue tunic embroidered with three mighty whirlwinds.

'Slow service,' he muttered. 'Can't abide it.'

'It really is most discourteous,' agreed Sir Politesse with a sniff, and Sir Palindrome added that he never could decide whether he liked the fast or the slow sort best.

'Well, where are the others?' demanded Sir Bivouac, waving a chicken leg in the air. 'Where's old Vortigern blown off to?'

'Not to mention Retty and Sluggy,' added Sir Dizziwind. 'Long names! Can't abide 'em.'

'Manners!' whistled Sir Politesse quietly to himself with a self-sacrificing air.

Eleanor was on the point of getting up from her corner and asking the knights whether there was any news of her mother, when she heard a great clanking and stamping from the door, and in came Sir Vortigern, Sir Reticule, and Sir Slugabed. She decided that, just for the moment, she would stay where she was, and watch what happened.

Sir Reticule was dropping bundles of hay and firewood right and left, while Sir Slugabed collapsed in a chair, exhausted. Sir Vortigern strode forward and threw down on the floor the great head of a beast. There it lay, its lips set in a snarl, while the firelight gleamed on its tusks.

'Well done, Vorty,' called out Sir Dizziwind. 'What sort of thing do you call that then, eh?'

'Manticore. Hard run, that, but I got it in the end. Devilish things, those: fight like furies, then flatter and coax when they're cornered.'

He sat himself down at the head of the table, and began pulling a chicken apart with great ceremony. When Master Richard came back with the candles, the chicken, and the ale, he was told to put more coal on the fire, and brew a big bowl of punch. Sir Vortigern let out a satisfied sigh.

'Pretty good day's sport, all in all. Met the Queen, too. Seeing the sights with her ladies. Dangerous idea.'

'Ah,' put in Sir Bivouac, pouring himself a cup of ale. 'You didn't hear, then. She's got herself lost in the woods. Everyone's out looking for her.'

'Who is?' asked Sir Slugabed, alarmed.

'Well, not *us*, obviously. We've won enough glory for today, don't you think?'

'Not our line,' agreed Sir Dizziwind. 'We're questers after beasts, not lookers for lost Queens.'

'No call to butt in.'

'Search is in able hands.'

'Whose hands?' wondered Sir Slugabed, yawning.

'Dunno. Peasants and things. Clever chaps.'

'Deserve our refreshment,' confirmed Sir Reticule.

'Earned it.'

'Mustn't strain ourselves.'

'Getting overtired. Fatal, sometimes.'

Just then the punch-bowl arrived. The knights' meal was over, the floor around was a mass of bones, and the table itself a blaze of light in the dark room.

'A toast!' called Sir Vortigern, reeling from his place. 'To Her Majesty! May she turn up one day, and not be too much worse for wear!'

'And I've another toast,' added Sir Politesse, swaying to his feet. 'To the fair Princess!'

They drank off their cups, while Sir Reticule murmured, 'And all who sail in her.'

Sir Vortigern fixed his companion with a stern eye. 'That is an Antediluvian Joke, Sir Reticule. Noah refused to let it on the Ark, but somehow it survived. For that, I'll oblige you to drink a bumper.'

'A bumper! A bumper!' the others called out, and a large cup was filled to the brim for Sir Reticule's punishment.

'I don't see why you're always in charge,' objected Sir Reticule. 'I'm the strongest: I carry the baggage!'

'But *I* am of the most ancient family,' replied Sir Vortigern, shocked. 'Why, do any of you others know the name of your great-great-great-great-great—'

A shrill laugh interrupted him. Sir Reticule quietly poured the contents of the bumper into a travelling-flask for later, while Sir Vortigern turned to glare at a group of goblins, in fits of giggles by the fire. One of them had put the coal-scuttle on its head, tucked the poker under one arm for a lance, and climbed up on another piggy-back.

'I am the brave Sir Vortigern!' shrieked the goblin, while a third stamped about breathing deep. 'Oh, my deary goodness me!' quivered the first goblin. 'It is a giant! But I am the brave Sir Vortigern, and I shall slay you and slay you and slay you until you're dead!'

Sir Vortigern turned pale with fury. 'I shall avenge this slur on my knighthood, caitiff goblin!' He drew his sword and leapt towards the capering group on the hearthstone. The goblins dived out of the way with squeaks, as the mighty sword came down and squashed the coal-scuttle completely out of shape.

'Take that!' yelled the goblin, jabbing the poker into Sir Vortigern's behind, and the knight replied by roaring and cleaving in two the table under which the goblin was hiding. Now Sir Dizziwind and Sir Bivouac sprang to his aid, smashing chairs and stools to splinters as they chased the goblins round the room.

Master Richard ran in. 'What's this! Stop, sirs, stop!'

'I'll catch it! For the sake—hic—of my ances—hic—tors, and the fair—hic—prinsick—Elihick—nor. Hic!' Sir Vortigern at last collapsed back on his chair, out of breath and hiccupping madly. The innkeeper chased away the goblins, with cries from the knights of 'Aye aye, skipper!' 'Thar she blows!' 'Belay that goblin!'

'The rascally creatures won't stay still!' complained the exasperated Sir Bivouac.

'Never mind them,' Sir Reticule reassured him. 'Ogres and dragons are more our line. Give us a clear run and a beast that'll stand and fight: that's when we prove our valour.'

'Small game, goblins,' agreed Sir Dizziwind. 'Hardly worth bothering with.'

'You're right,' said Sir Vortigern. 'A knight—hic—must be above such trifles. Gentlemen, to tomorrow!'

'To tomorrow!' chorused the others, and it was at that moment that Sir Politesse caught sight of Princess Eleanor, a dark cloaked shape in the corner.

'My dear sir!' called out the knight. 'Will you join us?'

'Why not share a bottle and a song with some bluff, simple chaps?' invited Sir Bivouac, and 'What's keeping you?' growled Sir Dizziwind. But Princess Eleanor could only gaze back in horror, and silently shook her head.

She was saved by a sound from out in the courtyard: shouts, and hoofbeats on the cobbles. Torchlight glared at the window, and a moment later in stepped the Queen.

She looked glassy-eyed and faint. Lady Linda and Lady Samantha were supporting her arms and dabbing at her forehead with scented handkerchiefs, while various members of the Royal Guard hovered anxiously round.

Eleanor sprang up from her place. 'Mother!'

'My dear,' murmured the Queen, while the knights fell over each other in amazement, staring from the lost Queen they hadn't helped to find, to the cloaked stranger who was a Princess.

'What happened?' Eleanor demanded, running up to her mother.

'Don't *ever* ask me that,' groaned the Queen, as she sank into a chair. She smiled feebly at the knights, who had now begun bowing and curtsying all over the place. 'Ah, brave Sir Vortigern. I've no doubt *you* managed very well, but I should have known better than to follow you into that den of . . . ' She shuddered. ' . . . *Witchcraft*!'

'Your servant, ma'am,' Sir Vortigern muttered, between bows.

Eleanor stared at her. 'Witchcraft? But you've always said the magic could only be good . . . the Lady of the Woods, you said . . . '

'I don't care! I've changed my mind. I've had enough: no more magic! Get rid of it!'

'No more magic, ma'am,' echoed Sir Vortigern respectfully.

'Get rid of it, Your Majesty,' agreed Sir Bivouac, still bowing.

'But, mother,' began the Princess again, 'how *can* you get rid of it? The Lady of the Woods only gave you one wish, and you've used it.'

'I don't know how!' moaned the Queen. 'Get rid of it, that's all!'

'That's all,' murmured Sir Vortigern, making another little bow, and wondering if it was safe to get back to the punch yet. But the Queen was staring hard in the direction of the knights, and her face was breaking into one of her smiles.

'Sir Vortigern! And *just* when the kingdom has need of you!'

Eleanor looked from the knights to her mother. She knew that look on her mother's face: it was the look of a new fad, and it usually meant bad news.

'It will be a great quest,' the Queen was saying. 'The greatest, perhaps, a knight has ever undertaken . . .'

Sir Vortigern unsheathed his sword and knelt before the Queen. 'Ma'am! This indeed is talk I love to hear! A quest, ma'am?'

'Indeed, sir knight! A *great* quest, to rid this realm of the foul pest of sorcery—'

'Mother!' Eleanor begged, with the horrible feeling that something awful was going to happen.

'Please, my dear. Don't interrupt. The quest to rid this land of the plague of Magic and Mystery . . . wilt thou undertake it, sir knight?'

The knights were kneeling and swearing and pulling out their swords as fast as each could manage.

'By my ancestors, ma'am, I swear it!'

'Another toast,' cried Sir Bivouac: 'to tomorrow!'

'When we shall do great things!'

'Slay dragons!'

'Brain giants!'

'And,' went on the Queen, 'for a great quest, a great prize. A proclamation will be sent through all the kingdom: to the brave knight who succeeds shall be given . . . the hand of the Princess Eleanor in marriage!'

'*Mother!*' screamed the Princess.

'Fear not!' Sir Vortigern assured Eleanor. '*I* shall be the one to win you!'

'Not if one of the rest of us beats you to it,' cautioned Sir Reticule.

'Quite!' sniffed Sir Politesse. 'Fair play to be observed at all times!'

'Ah, chivalry!' sighed the Queen. '*So* romantic!'

'But, mother, listen to me! I *won't* marry them. I won't!'

'Goodness me, my dear! Surely you don't *object*? What husband could be better? A handsome knight, in shining armour? Now do brace up, dear. You know a queen's word can't be taken back once it's given. At your age I'd have been *delighted*.'

Eleanor cast one look at the knights, who at the word 'handsome' had begun preening themselves and tossing their heads to show off their profiles. Then she looked at the Queen, smiling and rather puzzled, and she stormed out of the room.

CHAPTER 7

Prattlebox

Upstairs, Master Richard showed Eleanor to a bedchamber, but she didn't sleep. Instead, she paced her room furiously. Marry one of the knights! Never. The thought of them made her shiver: Sir Vortigern and his dots, Sir Bivouac with his tent, Sir Reticule, Sir Slugabed . . . No!

But she'd have to. It was true what her mother had said: a queen can't break her word. The proclamation will go out, one of the knights will succeed, and then it would be her duty. She paced back again, and cheered up a bit. They can't do it, she thought. Spells and beasts and goblins and ghosts—none of the knights could manage it . . . But could she be sure? And at the same time as hoping they couldn't do it, she hoped they could as well. *Someone* had to get rid of the magic. Her mother couldn't bear much more of it, and the kingdom was going to pot.

Eleanor stopped her pacing. She had to think. The magic had to go, but she couldn't leave it to the knights. That meant she would have to see to it herself. But how?

'I don't know anything about it,' she admitted to herself. 'I didn't even know about the different kinds of goblins, not like the boy at the mill . . . '

She reached in her pocket and took out the odd, goblin-faced coin, and then she smiled. She saw what to do.

Grey light was beginning to show at the windows.

Dawn wasn't far off: the moon had set, and already the mist was drifting apart in unwilling strands, hiding itself away for another night. Eleanor threw on her cloak and slipped down to the main room of the inn.

A couple of knights were snoring peacefully, their heads on the table, and there was the faint sound of goblins scampering in the wainscot. Eleanor took some food from the kitchen, leaving a coin in payment, and on her way back she met Master Richard.

'Up early, Your Highness. No one else astir, as yet.'

'And the Queen? She's still asleep too?'

'Asleep and under guard. A litter's been sent for to carry her back to the Castle—and more guardsmen, too, they say.'

Eleanor heaved a sigh of relief. That meant her mother should be safe—at least for a while.

'I'm riding out,' she told the innkeeper. 'Tell the Queen if she asks . . . tell her I've got something to do, and I'll be back when I've done it.' She gave Master Richard a smile, slipped away into the yard and saddled her horse, and was away west into the woods.

By the time she got to the mill the sun had risen. She paused for a moment on the edge of the clearing, unwilling to break the stillness, listening to the endless, lonely turning of the mill-wheel. Then the miller's son came out of the storehouse carrying a sack of grain, and smiled at her.

'You're back! Did your mother come home safe?'

'Yes, thank you,' answered the Princess. 'She was rather shaken, though. I never did find out quite what happened.'

'I've got a guess or two,' replied Tom, who dumped the sack in the mill and came out again. 'I know those trees and their tricks.'

'Who's there, Tom?' called out the miller from inside, and coming out caught sight of the Princess. 'Good morning to you, my fine young lady! A good day for a ride, indeed! Will you step up the hill and take a cup of buttermilk with mother?'

'You're very kind,' replied Eleanor, 'but what I really want is to have a word with your son, if you can spare him. I think he may be able to help me again.'

'Oh, surely, surely. I can spare him for such a cause as that.' And the miller took her bridle as she dismounted, tethered the horse, and went back inside.

'Now then, my lady,' Tom said. 'I'm all at your service, and ready to help you all I can.'

Princess Eleanor frowned, not knowing quite how to begin.

'Can we go somewhere we can't be overheard? Somewhere there aren't any goblins?'

Tom thought a moment. 'We could sit by the still pool below the falls: it's a place the goblins don't much like, and they couldn't hear anyhow, over the river.'

He led the way, wondering more and more. When they had sat down by the river bank, the Princess turned to him, and hesitated again. All her troubles seemed to whirl round her: the wish, the ring, the magic, the knights, the Queen's proclamation . . .

'I do so hope you can help me,' she began. 'Can I call you Tom? That's your name, isn't it?'

'It is indeed,' replied Tom, 'and you're welcome to call me by it.'

'My name's Eleanor.'

'Like the Princess?' said Tom.

'Yes.' Eleanor glanced down. 'Very like the Princess.'

'You *are* the Princess,' Tom stated, and Eleanor looked up again in distress, and nodded.

'It was all my mother's doing!' she burst out. 'Magic and Mystery! Why did she have to do it? Now I'll have to marry one of those awful, unspeakable knights, and I don't know who can help me, if you can't!'

'Wait a minute,' said Tom. 'Let's hear it all one thing at a time, and then we'll see what we can do.'

'All this magic,' began the Princess more calmly, 'all these pranks and hauntings and enchantments and beasts and bogeys, they all came about because the Lady of the Woods gave my mother a ring with a wish in it. I *told* her to save it up, but she wouldn't. And so she wished.'

'Magic and Mystery,' Tom repeated. 'That's what she wished for?'

Eleanor nodded. 'It's been nothing but nasty shocks for her from the start, but she would insist on seeing more and more. Goblins weren't enough, or ghosts, or beasts . . . but whatever it was she saw in the woods, that did it. She's had enough, and she wants to get rid of it.'

'Well, can't she just wish it away again?'

'The ring only had one wish in it. And now she's got the idea that the knights can do it for her, and whoever succeeds is to have my hand in marriage. And I think they're beasts, and I'd never marry any of them, but if they got rid of the magic then I'd have to. And you're the only one who knows the least thing about goblins and ghosts and things. Do *you* know how to get rid of it all?'

'Why, no,' admitted Tom, scratching his head. 'But don't give up: we'll see what we can make of it. Now I've been thinking a bit while you were speaking—'

'Have you?' asked Eleanor, her face lighting up.

'And the first thing that seems to me is this, that the

knights are part of the magic themselves. There's something not quite right about them, something outside nature, as there is with the goblins and everything else. And I don't believe the magic can be got rid of by something that's a part of it.'

Eleanor frowned again. 'Yes . . . but the risk's horrible. And someone's got to get rid of it.'

'Hold on,' said Tom. 'I'm still thinking. Next thing is this: the one to send the magic away is the one who brought us it in the first place. We'll have to find the Lady of the Woods. Then we tell her how upset the Queen is, and how she's changed her mind, and can she take it away again?'

Eleanor shook her head with a sigh. 'It was just a freak of chance, my mother saving her from the river in the floods. We could search the forest for years and never find her again.'

'That's true,' admitted Tom. 'I've never seen the Lady of the Woods, and I doubt if even grandmother has. But I think I might have an idea—'

'Yes?'

'It's this. You remember that bookworm goblin we saw in the clearing? Now, it's my belief that a goblin like that might know a great deal, and if we caught one, it could tell us something of use. It would have to answer our questions, you see, or we'd never let it go.'

'And you're just the one for catching goblins!' cried the Princess. 'Oh, I knew I could rely on you!' She jumped up. 'When do we start?'

'Why, right now!' said Tom, jumping up too.

They made their way back to the mill. Tom fetched from the storehouse a net, some weights, and some rope, and ran home for his book of ballads, which was an important part of his plan. Then he led the Princess back through the woods to the clearing where they had first seen the talkative bookworm.

'The thing I don't understand,' said Princess Eleanor, as they approached the glade, 'is what the book of ballads is for.'

'It's bait,' Tom explained. 'Most goblins go for food, but it stands to reason you should use a book to trap a bookworm. I'm afraid ballads may not suit its taste, but it's the only book I've got, so it'll have to do.'

When the pair got to the clearing they set to work on the trap. Eleanor laid the net out on the ground between a couple of large greenish toadstools and covered it over with some of last year's leaves, while Tom tied ropes on all round, and led them over the ground and up to the branch of a tree, where he tied them to the weights.

After that, there was nothing to do but crouch in the bushes and wait for a goblin. Eleanor thought of all that would have to happen before she was safe from the clutches of the knights: the goblin trapped, the Lady of the Woods found, and the magic banished; while Tom, keeping a tight grip on the rope that would spring the trap, thought what a funny business it was doing a good turn to a princess, and there she was hiding in a bush with him when she could be in the Castle surrounded by pages and footmen by the dozen.

They waited a long time. At last, they saw a pair of goblins frisking up, leap-frogging over each other. They stopped to glance at the book, and capered off with scornful remarks about how much they hated such things.

'*They're* not bookworms,' whispered the Princess.

'Quiet!' hissed Tom. 'Look!'

Ambling into the clearing came the short, untidy figure of the bespectacled bookworm. It stooped over the book, and the next moment it had picked it up and was scowling at it in disappointment. Tom yanked on the rope, the weights swished off the branch into the bushes, and the bookworm was swinging in the air.

'Disreticulate me incontinently!' bellowed the goblin.

Tom, who was laughing, said, 'It's no use speaking in goblin-talk. Can't you make yourself understood?'

'Well, get me out of this net right now, then!' yelled the goblin.

'Do you think we should do that?' asked Tom of the Princess.

'Well, we might,' she replied playfully, 'but if we do, I think we should tie its tail to something so it doesn't run away. Don't you?'

'Oh, I think that's an excellent idea!' agreed Tom, hauling down the struggling bundle of goblin and tying the creature's tail firmly to the root of a tree. 'There we are!'

'Oh, I disesteem you both most fervently!' exclaimed the goblin. 'And oh, how profoundly I loathe and contemn all knots and entanglements, all bends and all hitches!'

'Well, we'll untie you when you've done something for us,' said Tom.

'If you want my gold it's no good,' declared the goblin, 'because we intellectual goblins don't have any.'

'It's not gold we want. It's answers. And if you don't tell the truth I'll put you in my big cage, and never let you go.'

'Oh, not the big cage, master!' pleaded the goblin. 'I'll answer truly, I swear it by the Prince of Hobgoblins himself!'

'Very well then,' said Tom. 'First of all, what's your name?'

'Prattlebox.'

'You say you're an intellectual,' pursued the Princess. 'Does that mean the same as intelligent?'

At this, the goblin ground its teeth and squinted horribly, but it was too frightened not to tell the truth, so at last it said, 'No! It doesn't!'

'But you do know things?' went on Eleanor.

'Obviously,' sniffed Prattlebox. 'You see, whereas most goblins are born with a purse of gold and no sense at all between their pointed ears, intellectual goblins are born having read books. Don't ask me where or how, but I'd read books already when I was nothing more than a seed. So yes, I know rather a lot, actually.'

'Then tell us about the Lady of the Woods,' ordered Tom. 'You know about her, too?'

'I am acquainted with the personage to whom you allude,' retorted the goblin smugly.

'And do you know where she lives?'

Prattlebox made a face. 'Yes and no. I fancy you hardly understand what you're asking.'

'What do you mean?' said Eleanor.

'I mean, dear lady, that the Lady of the Woods generally does not live in any one place for longer than a day, and if you asked me to tell you what her house looked like, I would have to give you a hundred different answers, none of which you would believe.'

'Well, what *does* it look like?' asked Tom. 'Explain it to us, if you know so much about it.'

'Simply this. Every day her house takes on a new form and a new size. Sometimes it appears as a great castle in the clouds, and you can see it towering above the sun as it sets. Sometimes it is tiny, a miniature palace set in its estate and grounds, the whole thing floating on a lily-pad in a still pool. Then again it might be a snail's shell, or a pine cone, or even a cuckoo-clock in a poor cottage, and one of her favourite shapes is a bees' nest, hanging from the branch of an old oak tree deep in the woods. It's always changing and always moving, and always looks like something it isn't, and always has a labyrinth of rooms inside, where the Lady stores her treasures and her magic.'

'But it must be possible to find her somehow,' objected the Princess.

'It is possible, yes. But only if you use magic: and the task is full of danger. Are you ready for that?'

The Princess looked at Tom, who looked at the goblin, and answered, 'Yes.'

'Very well then. You must cut a wand and make it magic. Then, if you hold the wand and speak certain words which I shall tell you, you will at once be changed to whatever size the Lady of the Woods has assumed on that particular day. Next, you must touch some creature, whether beast or bird, with the wand, and repeat the same magic words. That creature will at once make its way to her house. All you have to do is follow it: ride on it, fly with it, or whatever. At sunset, you will return to your normal size.'

The goblin surveyed the human pair, both somewhat overawed and sunk in thought. 'That's silenced you,' gloated Prattlebox. 'There's more thinking-fodder in your trough than you looked to find there!'

'Quiet, goblin,' said Tom sternly. 'Tell us how to make the wand.'

'Now that's *wood* magic,' went on Prattlebox in a tone of satisfaction, 'and there aren't many goblins who understand how that works. It all follows a different principle, you see: not that I want to blind you laymen with science, of course, but goblin magic all goes by sevens. Seven syllables to the line in our spells, seven times seven to make an enchantment, and so on. Now wood magic isn't the same at all: that works by nines.'

'Yes,' interrupted Tom, 'but how do we make the wand?'

'I was circumlocuting in that direction,' sniffed Prattlebox. 'The spell, you see, is a *wood* spell. You must cut a willow wand and take it to some still water where the blue of the sky is reflected. That is most important. The blue gets into the water, you see, and from there into the wand. Dip the wand nine times in the water, and each time you must repeat these words:

> 'O willow wand, O wand of willow,
>> be my guide:
>> let me ride
>> beast and bird
>> by you spurred,
>> and be kind
>> till I find
> where'er the Lady's head doth pillow.

'You will observe,' the goblin went on, 'that the first and last lines are of nine syllables, with nine and nine between. I read all that in the same book.

'The words are the same when you wish to change your size, and the same when you wish to enchant an animal to seek out the habitation the Lady of the Woods. And now, if you've quite finished with me, I wonder if you might disembroil my caudal appendage— that is, untie my tail, so that I may commence a stylometric analysis of this volume of (if I may say so) rather vulgar and frivolous poetry which I found lying on the ground.'

Tom released the goblin's tail, and Eleanor, her mind

already on the quest, said rather dreamily, 'Thank you, Prattlebox.'

'Don't mention it,' snapped the goblin, tugging its tail from Tom's grasp. Before he could stop it, Prattlebox had lurched off across the clearing between the toadstools. It had the book of ballads open in its paw, and was muttering, 'Ha! Atrocious style!'

'My book!' shouted out Tom. 'Come back here: that's my only book!'

'I'll get you another,' cried the Princess. 'Come on! Let's find the Lady of the Woods!'

CHAPTER 8

A Wand of Willow

Eleanor ran ahead down to the river. By the time Tom caught up, she was already among the willow bushes by the bank, pulling down pliant shoots and testing them.

'Here! How about this one?'

Tom drew his knife, and the wand was cut.

'Come on, then!' urged the Princess, and picked her way down to the water's edge. The sun was high by now. Below the falls the blue of the sky fell full on the pool, gently rippled out in the middle of the stream, and pure and still by the banks.

Tom followed more slowly, sat himself beside her, and dipped the wand in the water. The breeze dropped, and all the forest seemed to be listening and watching as he said the words. Again he said the spell, and again: nine times in all, and then he looked at the Princess and smiled.

'Well?' she asked. 'Did it work? Is it magic?'

'I think so,' said Tom, turning the wand in his hand. 'It seems lighter than before, and I could feel the water tugging at it somehow, soaking up into it maybe. But now it's quite dry.'

'That must have been the blue of the sky, just like Prattlebox told us. Come on, then! How soon do we start?'

At this, Tom looked more serious. 'I think, Princess, that I should really go alone.'

'Go alone? Why should you go alone?'

'Well, I'm used to the woods, and it isn't right for you to run any risks.'

'But it isn't any righter for you to run them,' argued Eleanor. 'And I've really got to be there to explain things to the Lady of the Woods. It was my mother who started it all. You do see that, don't you? And besides, I've made up my mind.'

Tom frowned, thinking of the malice of the trees, the bellowing beasts and the mocking echo, and all the other perils of the woods.

'Dear Princess, it's too dangerous. I really can't let you.'

'But you'll really have to, dear Tom,' Eleanor replied, and plucked the wand from his hand.

'O willow wand, O wand of willow,' she began, and was already starting to shrink when Tom caught hold of the wand as well, and blurted the spell out as quickly as he could.

Now it went in a whirl, and the two of them shrank together, down and down. They felt as if they were falling from a great height hand in hand; the air rushed and their bodies lightened, and just as they expected to hit the ground hard, they drifted lightly down on to a soft bed of earth, dazed but safe.

'Where are we?' gasped Eleanor, looking all round. Nothing was familiar. The river had gone, and so had the woods and the grassy river bank; instead, they were standing on a bare plain, with roundish boulders dotted about that towered over their heads. Between these rose the pale stalks of giant plants, stretching off into a matted forest on every side.

'I think we're in just the same place,' said Tom, frowning harder than ever.

'But we can't be! Look at all those . . . *things*!'

Up above ran a maze of roadways, all a burning, brilliant green, arching high and overlapping in a thousand crossroads, and shifting all the time in the wind. And on these roads there were creatures, from the size of a sheep to that of a coach-and-four, their bodies yellow or blue or shining gold, their many legs probing on like careful walking-sticks.

'They're giant insects,' concluded Eleanor in disgust.

'No,' said Tom. 'I think they're just plain ordinary insects. We're the ones who are tiny people.'

Eleanor sat down against a pebble-boulder, and gazed up at the great green roadways. She could see it now. They were blades of grass.

'Oh, Tom! What are we going to do?'

'Well!' said Tom. 'We'll climb up among the grass and wait for a good, tame-looking insect to come along, and then we'll enchant it!'

So they began to climb one of the steep, slippery grass-stalks. It was hard going at first, but the blade soon began to curve over, and then they could walk quite comfortably along the furrow down its middle.

'Just what do you call a tame-looking insect?' enquired the Princess, glancing down at a bright red beetle with striped feelers. 'I won't ride on just anything, you know.'

'Well, I'll try my best to find one worthy to carry a princess,' said Tom with a smile, 'but out here in the backwoods it might not be easy.'

They crept to the edge of the grass-blade and peered over. Below, an ant the size of a large bull was crawling by. A tiny flea, no bigger than a small dog, hopped along after it, while overhead a ladybird crept higher and higher, a great red dome on legs. Then Tom jogged Eleanor's arm.

'There! Look!'

He pointed to a fat, green bug, about the size of a pony.

'That!' exclaimed the Princess in distaste. 'Why, it looks like . . . like . . . a puffed-up balloon on legs! Do you really think we have to?'

'I think so,' Tom replied.

'Well, if you really do . . . '

They stood hand in hand on the edge of the grass-blade, while the insect crept closer below.

'Now!' Tom shouted. They jumped, and floated down to land with a hollow thud on the animal's back. Its six legs bent at the knees, its balloon-like body squashed in with the shock, and then they had bounced off, and their hands parted.

Eleanor landed with a jar, and found herself on bare earth, beside a towering pebble. She stood up and looked round for Tom, and then she heard his voice, low and frightened.

'Eleanor! Princess! Come quickly!'

She turned and ran up a small bank of earth, and stopped dead. A thing like a giant fishing-net stretched in front of her, with sparkling beads of dew hanging at the joins, and Tom lying still at its edge. But this was no net: its strands did not run straight. Instead, they led in towards the middle, where crouched a monstrous form. Eight pointed legs rested gently on the web, with a bulbous body looming up behind, and eight shining eyes were fixed on Tom.

'Help me!'

Tom shifted, trying to pull free, but the sticky threads held him fast, and he could not even move his arms. His struggles sent tremors along the web, and the spider ran at him. At the same moment Eleanor dived forward and snatched the wand from Tom's belt. It came up and met the creature's jaws just as they were lowering over their prey, and the spider stopped, spellbound.

The giant thing stood motionless over them, while Eleanor faltered out the words of the spell. Then, forgetting its dinner and its home, the spider turned and pattered off through the grass, with nothing on its mind but to reach the house of the Lady of the Woods.

Eleanor collapsed sobbing on the ground, and Tom had to wait until she had finished before asking her to cut him free.

'All right,' she said, pulling herself together and hacking at the strands. 'I'm better now. But you never said it would be like this!'

'I did say it would be dangerous.'

'Dangerous, yes,' replied the Princess reproachfully. 'But you never mentioned horrific, or appalling, or awful, or any of the other things it's been. I wouldn't have minded if it had just been dangerous, and that had been the end of it.'

'You saved my life, anyway,' said Tom. 'And you were right about that balloon-insect. That's no way to travel.'

'No way at all,' agreed the Princess. 'Well, what do we do next?'

'Next I think you should be in charge for a while. That spider's left me feeling a bit strange.'

'All right,' said the Princess. 'Then let's have lunch.' They climbed up into a tussock of grass for safety, and Eleanor unpacked the bundle of food from the inn. They finished off their meal with part of a huge wild strawberry, bigger than both of them, and sat back debating what to do.

'We must think,' said Tom. 'What's the best animal for the job?'

Below them, a gigantic snail was oozing slowly over the ground, a slimy dragon carrying a shell as big as a house.

'Something fast,' said Eleanor. 'It could be a long way, and we've used a lot of the day already. I didn't expect we'd be this long.'

'Well, what about a butterfly?'

Eleanor shook her head. 'With our luck, we'd be bound to fall off. Listen! What's that?'

It sounded like some large animal moving through the undergrowth, and a moment later a hare sprang out in front of them. It nosed about among the grass, nibbling this and that, and then it moved towards their tussock, attracted by the smell of the strawberries growing right beside it.

'A hare wouldn't eat a shrunken person, would it?' Eleanor whispered.

'Only by accident.'

'Wait a minute . . . that's it!'

'What?'

'We don't have to use a tiny animal just because *we're* tiny. Quick, while it's still eating!'

They edged silently along a stalk of grass until they were hanging right over the back of the hare, and then they let go. They landed in a forest of fur, and slipped down to the animal's warm, pink skin. Tom touched it with the wand, and with the last word of the spell the hare was off.

On it sped, leaping fallen trees and covering grassy glades faster than a greyhound, while Tom and Eleanor nestled like fleas, feeling the motion and seeing nothing. At last the animal made a final leap and stopped, sitting up on its haunches.

'We must be there,' whispered Tom, and Eleanor crept

up through the fur until she could look down the hare's back, stretching in a long curve to the ground.

'One last slide!' she cried, and jumped. Tom followed, and they rolled, slipped, and tumbled together to the earth. They picked themselves up, and saw confronting them a pair of creatures their own size, dressed in green, with graceful wings sprouting from their backs.

'Goblins?' whispered the Princess.

'I don't think so,' Tom whispered back. 'Something finer . . . I think they're elves.'

The creatures beckoned to them, and Tom and Eleanor followed. In front of them rose a towering hedgerow, rich with dog rose and honeysuckle; but at its foot, grotesque and out of season, grew a clump of villainous-looking toadstools. The elves headed straight for a dark opening among their stems, and disappeared inside.

Under the shade of the great domed caps Tom and Eleanor hesitated, unsure. And then they gathered their courage and stepped into the darkness.

CHAPTER 9

The Lady of the Woods

They found the two green-clad creatures waiting for them.

'You'll understand,' one of them said. 'This is indeed the Lady's house, and it's clear enough you seek her. Come.'

And their guides led them off, down tunnels and up winding, spiral stairs. A reddish light filtered in through the caps of the toadstools, and as they went Tom and Eleanor heard a murmuring and a whispering from the hundred rooms of the Lady's house. In some they saw illusions, tangled stairs reaching up and up, or mirrors reflecting them back an infinity of times; in others dreams lay asleep, and from others again they heard the murmur of slow Enchantments, repeating some powerful verse perhaps nine hundred and ninety-nine times, whispering on for years until the magic was done.

At last, by many turns, they were led to a broad hall, and there before them was the Lady. She was sitting by a kind of twisted window, gazing sadly out over the meadow, where the mist of evening was already beginning to gather, while by her side lay an abandoned pile of half-woven spells. She turned to them with a smile and a sigh.

'You are welcome here,' she said, and beckoned them to sit down while her elves brought them food. 'And now at least I understand the meaning of the spider which came to see me earlier. You have a Wand of

Finding. So one mystery at least is solved, and in these unlucky times the fewer mysteries the better.'

'That's just what we want to see you about,' said Princess Eleanor, rather uneasily. 'You see, when my mother, the Queen, wished for Magic and Mystery, she didn't really know quite what it would be like, and she's kept having nasty shocks. And ghosts and goblins probably suit some people, but she's found out that she's not that sort. And now she doesn't think she wants it any more, and I know it sounds ungrateful, but will you take it away again?'

The Lady of the Woods looked sadder than ever at this, and slowly shook her head. Eleanor was sure she had offended her.

'No, I don't think your mother ungrateful. Certainly I would take the Magic and Mystery away again—if only I could.'

Here Tom and Eleanor looked at each other in alarm and puzzlement.

'Yes,' the Lady went on. 'The magic has gone wrong, every bit of it. My spells are twisted; the wrong beasts galloped from the Book of Wonders, not stags and unicorns but manticores and yales, strange things with moon-eyes and cloven feet; and my Golden Horn woke malice and spite, and left beauty still asleep. And likewise the rest: elves and flowers and dreams have grown into goblins, toadstools, nightmares.'

Eleanor stared. 'And the knights—did you summon them too?'

'Those ones? No. I called Galahad and Lancelot, valiant and strong and true. And instead who came? Reticule and Slugabed, foolish and vain, and seven instead of nine. Seven, always seven! The number of goblins, and the moon; and under the eye of the moon all the enchantments breathe stronger.

'And there was worse. When I set myself to struggle with this new magic, I found I had no power; and the strength of the moon was growing. So I turned my house to a toadstool, a form in which none would know it, and took myself away to think.'

'And what did you find out?'

'At first, nothing. I only knew that each of my spells had failed. But what did they have in common? My elf-seed, which failed to grow true to stock, my Book, my Horn . . . and then I knew. My wand: my wand of wood magic, which I must use to set the seal on any of my spells. And at the same time I saw the spider that sits at the middle of all this web of witchcraft. It is the Enchanter! The Bold Enchanter of the Moon!'

Eleanor felt a tingle run up her spine. 'So there *is* such a person . . . '

'Go on,' said Tom. 'What did he do?'

'This wand,' said the Lady of the Woods, holding it up, 'is not the one I made over long summer days, hardened in the winter frosts, and painted in the rainbows of spring. No! This is a twig of some barren thorn-thicket from the mountains of the moon, wrapped in illusions to deceive me. My own wand is gone—stolen. And the Enchanter's imps have left me this in its place.'

'But why?' demanded Eleanor. 'What good would it do him to swap the two wands?'

'A wood wand is useless to him, except as a treasure to hoard and boast of. But a moon wand placed in my hands and hidden in illusion is to the Enchanter a powerful weapon. He hoped, doubtless, that I might work some great magic with it, and thus increase his power on Earth. And so, indeed, it has come about.'

The Lady of the Woods let the wand fall with a sigh.

'This wand,' Tom began, 'the one that was stolen: if you had it back, could you put the magic to rights?'

'I could—if I had it.'

'But can't you get it back?' asked Eleanor. 'Or make another?'

'To make another would take nine times nine years. And while I would gladly set about the task, by the time I had finished the Enchanter would be master of us all. Power is his only love. He cannot come where the creatures of earth and air live: they are not his element. But if he can bring the Earth to share in the cheesy, moony nature of his home, then he could come here freely, and not just look out over us by night.'

'Then it means a trip to the moon to get back the wand?' Tom said.

The Lady nodded gravely. 'But that is something I can never do, for the same reason the Enchanter cannot come here. The moon, you see, is beyond my element.'

There was silence a moment.

'But how *would* someone reach the moon?' Eleanor asked. 'Supposing they were going?'

'To reach the moon is not hard, for one with the courage to try. I have a powder, which must be sprinkled over the head of a horse. By its magical virtue, the horse would then sprout wings and carry you wherever you wish. There are meteors and comets to pass, and drifts of stardust, but those are not the worst hazards. Once on the moon, the Enchanter must be found and defeated, and he is powerful in his own country.'

'But it must be possible,' said Tom, turning it all over in his mind.

'Yes,' said the Lady of the Woods. 'It is possible, because, if you go, I shall give you this.' And she handed him the moon wand.

Tom took it hesitatingly. 'Really? But—isn't this wand very powerful?'

'It is. But the Enchanter can only be defeated by his own magic: I have no power in this fight at all. If you learn to use that wand and to cast the spells of moon magic, you can be his equal; also, you will have the benefit of surprise, for he would never expect me to give away the only wand I have.'

Tom drew in his breath and stood up.

'Well then, since someone's got to go, it might as well be me. And the sooner I start the better.'

The Lady of the Woods regarded him steadily.

'If you undertake this journey, Tom the miller's son, you must know that you run a great risk. If you fail, you will be turned into an earwig, or worse, and live out the rest of your days scavenging for cheese scraps in the tunnels beneath the Enchanter's Castle.'

'I won't fail,' Tom said. 'Tell me if there's anything else I need to know.'

'You may trust the lowland Moonmen,' said the Lady. 'They are hardworking and honest, and the Enchanter's enemies. Some of them may be able to train you in moon magic. But do not trust the wild Moonmen of the Mountains, and above all things, never trust the Enchanter. Do not stare too long at the moon on your flight, or you will become moonsick, and on no account drink water that the moonshine has fallen on. You will find the moon a place of many wonders. Trust to yourself, and I think you may be safe.'

There was silence. Outside, the sun was sinking over the woods. Eleanor tugged at Tom's arm.

'It's time we were going. We'll be growing back to our normal size soon.'

The Lady of the Woods stood up, and an elf brought Tom a leather pouch containing the magic powder.

'Take these also,' said the Lady, dropping three stones into his hand. 'One is a lodestone; grip it in your hand, and you will be drawn to the thing you most desire. The next is a star-topaz, for healing the madness of the moon, if any be that unlucky, and the third is an emerald, a charm by which you may know the true from the false, for if a lie is uttered in its hearing, the stone burns hot for shame.'

Then the elf guided them back through the house, and the last they saw of the Lady was her smile, which now was brightened by hope.

CHAPTER 10

The Eagle's Flight

Tom and Eleanor followed the elf through the winding passages and down the long stairs in silence. Back in the green jungle of the meadow, the last rays of the sun fell on the grass stems over their heads. Then with a dizzying lurch their fingers stretched and their heads shot up, and they were back to their normal size. Now the grass was soft underfoot, and ahead they could see a stile leading out of the meadow and into a lane.

'I know this lane,' said Tom. 'If we follow it, we'll get to the Eagle. I need to speak to Master Richard about borrowing a horse.'

Princess Eleanor gave him a sidelong look. 'I believe you really think you're going to the moon by yourself.'

'Eh?' said Tom, who had been deep in thought. 'Yes, I do.'

'Well, you're not,' replied the Princess, in the same careless tone.

'Please, my dear Princess—' began Tom.

'Why do you always call me "dear Princess" when you're about to contradict me? If you're going to be troublesome, you should call me "Hey, mush!" and have done with it.'

'But,' Tom protested, 'two on one horse?'

'We'll just have to find a big one, won't we?'

At that moment they came to the inn. The first stars were out; mist was gathering over the fields, and off in the east the moon was rising, yellow and full. Inside the Eagle the knights were sitting round a roaring fire with their punch-bowl already in place, reckoning up the day's glorious deeds.

'Two more manticores to Sir Vortigern, at five points each,' Sir Politesse was saying. 'Still ahead, I fear.' Then Tom burst in, with Princess Eleanor right behind.

'You're just not thinking of the risk!' Tom said.

'There you go again!' Eleanor retorted. 'Why's it better for you to take risks than it is for me? Always treating me as if I'm special!'

'Well, you are. You're a princess, and I'm just a miller's son.'

'If that's so, you ought to do as I tell you. And anyway, you're not just the miller's son: you're Tom. What will your parents do if you're turned into an earwig? And you will be, if I'm not there to keep an eye on you.'

Meanwhile, the knights were tumbling from their chairs in amazement, and Sir Reticule had fallen over backwards under the weight of his rucksack.

'Your Royal Highness!' exclaimed Sir Vortigern, and Sir Politesse executed the most perfect bow he had ever made. It began at the tips of his toes and worked its way all up along his spine, until his whole body bent like a sapling and his forelock skimmed the floor.

'There, you see,' said Princess Eleanor, pointing to the knight, who was having some difficulty unbending himself again. 'That's how I ought to be treated: with respect!'

'Royal Princess,' began Sir Vortigern fiercely, 'willingly would I lay down my life to avenge thine honour on any who violated thy Royal dignity and estate.'

'Please keep out of this,' said Eleanor, and turned back to Tom. 'Is it because I'm a girl? Because I'm much quicker than you are, and you know it. And besides—'

'Where's Master Richard?' demanded Tom of Sir Reticule, who had now picked himself up and was helping Sir Politesse to straighten his backbone.

'What's it to you, miller's boy?' retorted Sir Reticule. 'He's upstairs making beds. Why don't you go and help him?'

'Making beds!'

'We can't all be early risers,' said Sir Politesse reproachfully. 'Try to have some understanding of your fellow man!'

Tom strode off towards the stairs, and Eleanor went after him.

'Lady,' intoned Sir Vortigern, 'if this rude fellow hath offered thee affront—'

'Can't you keep out of this?' cried Eleanor, and ran up the stairs after Tom. She followed the sound of sheets being shaken out, and found both him and the innkeeper in a chamber overlooking the front of the inn.

'Master Richard, can I borrow a horse?'

The innkeeper looked up in surprise to see first Tom, then Princess Eleanor, and then a gaggle of knights.

'Wants to borrow a horse!' guffawed Sir Reticule. 'Going to be a knight like us, eh?'

'Pack-beast for bags of flour, most likely,' commented Sir Bivouac; but Sir Vortigern advanced on Tom threateningly.

'Sirrah, I have sworn myself the protector of this fair and Royal lady, and I know not what devilry thou mayest be plotting—'

'He's going to fly to the moon,' shouted Princess Eleanor, 'and he's leaving me behind!'

At this, the knights burst into roars of laughter, and even Master Richard looked puzzled.

'Fly to the moon on a millstone, miller's boy!' Sir

Reticule taunted him. 'Going to grind it up for flour? Always wondered what happened to the dear old thing each month!'

'It's true!' shouted Tom, now angry at last. 'I have a powder here which will make a horse sprout wings and fly.' And he held up the pouch and waved it at the knights. 'And if you'll only lend me a horse, Master Richard, I promise it'll very probably lose its wings again when I come back, and if it doesn't you can sell it for a profit.'

'Why, Master Tom, I don't know,' the innkeeper began, and 'Look out, Tom!' shouted the Princess, for Sir Bivouac had rushed forward and grabbed the leather pouch from Tom's hands.

'What have we here? You'd better take a look, Sir Baggage-Train!' As Tom made a snatch, Sir Bivouac tossed the pouch across to Sir Reticule, who was standing by the window.

'Handy pouch,' he remarked. 'Come in useful for carrying something or other. We don't need this powder, though.' And before Tom could reach him, Sir Reticule had emptied the pouch out of the window.

Tom looked out vainly after the powder, then turned on Sir Reticule, while Princess Eleanor stamped in frustration, and elbowed Sir Vortigern in the stomach as he attempted to escort her downstairs. Sir Bivouac was still chuckling when Tom fetched Sir Reticule a blow on the nose that brought him to the floor, where he lay on his rucksack, bawling for help.

There is no telling how this ugly scene might have developed, if a very strange thing had not then happened. From outside, down below the window, there came a creaking sound, like mighty timbers stretching and grating on each other, and then a deafening screech cut through the night air for miles around, and was echoed back in many different voices by the rocks and crags. Tom and the Princess ran to the window, and there beneath them was the old oak post, carved in the shape of an eagle. The enchanted powder had fallen full on it. Great wooden wings were unfolding from its flanks, the length of the inn and beyond. The eagle's head turned from side to side; its carved beak opened, showing a wooden tongue, and let out another ear-piercing shriek. The wings flexed and swept the air, and in another moment they were tipped backwards off their feet, as the inn gave a bound and lifted itself into the sky.

'What is it? What is it?' panted Sir Bivouac, who picked himself up and ran to a window, only to see the lights of the village dwindling below, and his own camp in its moonlit field, fast shrinking in size.

'Let me up, oh do let me up!' pleaded Sir Reticule. 'I'll say I'm sorry!'

Sir Vortigern's face bulged with astonishment, and Tom and Eleanor collapsed together in fits of laughter. In a single moment their quarrel was over and their journey begun, the powder was not lost after all, and the knights looked very ridiculous.

The next to speak was Master Richard. 'Now then, it seems to me it's like this. We're on a voyage, my lads, and we're bound for the moon. I'm an old seafaring man, and fit enough to be captain of any vessel, to my way of thinking. This is my inn, and my ship, and I'll have it run tight. So all the grog goes under lock and key, and you knights can sort yourselves into watches, and report for orders.'

Sir Politesse flowed with promises and apologies, while nudging his friends viciously in the ribs. In the end Sir Vortigern muttered out, 'Aye aye, Captain!' and the knights shuffled out of the room, defeated.

The inn was rising up through the mist, which curled and whispered past the windows, forming itself into soft fists that rapped at the panes, or pale fingers that tried the hinges and catches. The Eagle flew with strong, slow downward beats of its wings, so that every few seconds the building lurched suddenly higher into the air. This motion was too much for some of the knights, who very soon became innsick, and tottered out on to the gallery overlooking the inn yard for some fresh air. The stables adjoining the inn had flown up with the rest, and the horses were still inside, whinnying with fright; but instead of the comforting square of cobbles between them and the inn, there was only an empty void, with the hills and fields lying ever further below in the blue moonlight.

Goblins ran through the house in excitement, calling to each other and pointing to the moon, high above over the Eagle's beak. The floor swayed like the deck of the ship, and the old inn's great oak timbers creaked and strained. Master Richard said the sounds reminded him of his days at sea, and he looked happier than Tom had ever seen him.

Up and up the inn rose, and now and again its screech rang out through the night. Once they passed a group of Nightmares, flapping slowly down the valley out of the woods, but the Eagle's scream frightened them, and they turned and skulked back to their hiding places.

They were higher than the hills now; the river lay below like a silver thread, and then disappeared into the darkness. The air grew colder, and drifts of silvery clouds could be seen off on either side. Tom had noticed as the sun was setting a long strip of cloud trailing upwards to the east, and now the Eagle set its course along it, while the moon still rode high in the distance ahead, cold and bright. Tom and Eleanor sat together in silence by the window as the ribbon of silver mist unfurled beneath them and the inn creaked gently on its way.

'Don't stare at the moon,' Eleanor cautioned, and Tom jerked himself out of his reverie. He had been exploring in his imagination all the plains and valleys of that strange country they were so soon to visit, trying to make out on the moon's face the rugged Cheddar Mountains, and the Castle of the Bold Enchanter. The eye of the night was staring back on him, and its white light was oozing into his mind by all its cracks and joints, until it would have broken down the sluices and poured in, flooding his senses and drowning his reason.

'There, I've done you one good turn already,' said the Princess. 'You couldn't really have been such a beast as to leave me behind?'

'No, I suppose not,' said Tom, relenting with a smile. 'I can't deny you're a handy lass.'

'Well, I've never been called *that* before,' replied Princess Eleanor primly.

'Oh, thy pardon, modom,' said Tom, mimicking Sir Politesse's bow. 'Hath I offendedeth thy Highneth'th honour?'

'No breeding,' said the Princess, with the usual twinkle in her eye. 'None whatever. Oh well, never mind. Of course if Sir Galahad had turned up . . .'

Time passed, and now they had left even the highest clouds far behind. Swirls of stardust blew by and caught in the eaves, and Sir Bivouac and Sir Dizziwind were sent up to the top garret to keep an eye out for meteors. The Earth had shrunk to a darkened globe below,

94

showing them remote seas and strange lands, distant by many months' journey from their own, dimly lit in the moonlight. Ahead the moon was growing, and its plains and mountains were beginning to stand out clearly. Its light was stronger than ever now; it washed in at the windows and over walls, floors, and people, who had become like silver statues moving in a silver temple.

Suddenly a howling broke out that floated up from all around them like a hymn to the moon. Eleanor shivered.

'What's that?'

Tom shook his head, when the captain ran in. ''Tis more mischief,' he complained. 'The knights again: they drank from the water-butt that stands below the gallery, and now they're plain moonsick, and can do nothing but howl and howl like lonely wolves.'

'Let me see.' Tom and Eleanor went down to the main room of the inn, and there by the window were Sir Vortigern, Sir Palindrome, and Sir Politesse, howling at the moon as if their lives depended on it.

'Moonshine,' said Tom, and then remembered his grandmother's rhyme. 'They're loons that sing to the moon, and the moon laughs back at them for their pains. Well, we mustn't have a moonsick crew aboard.' He took from his pocket the golden star-topaz the Lady had given him, and forced the hand of each knight in turn to close around it. At once they recovered their senses, and slunk sheepishly off in different directions.

On they flew, while Tom and Eleanor returned to the front chamber to look at the passing night scene. The air outside was bitterly cold; comets whisked past like giant sparks, flicking their tails and casting a momentary yellow glare into the room. Then, suddenly, the look-outs up in the garret set up a great shout.

'What are you waiting for?' cried Sir Dizziwind. 'It's meteors! Left, I tell you, left!'

'What's this?' demanded the captain. 'A cry of reefs, is it?'

'Aye aye,' replied Tom, and they all peered ahead. Sure enough, up ahead the air was surging around a cluster of rocks that floated in the sky, turning slowly and catching the light of the moon on one broken surface after the other.

'Two points to larboard,' cautioned Master Richard, and Tom took up a warming-pan and touched the Eagle twice on its left shoulder. The great bird responded at once, and he soon found this was an easy way of steering. And now, with Master Richard at his elbow, Tom guided the Eagle through narrow waters, where meteors lay in shoals on either side. The great wings beat slowly, lifting the inn gently between them, threading this way and that. At last the reefs were left behind and a great expanse of dark blue lay before them like a sea, with drifts of stardust heaped against the meteors at its edge like a beach of pale sand. The moon shone large and bright straight ahead.

'A clear run now,' said Master Richard, and became the innkeeper again. Off he went, and fetched back pies and sausages and moderate measures of ale for all hands. Tom and Eleanor ate almost in silence, looking now at each other, now for a moment at the moon ahead. When they had finished, Master Richard turned and spoke to them.

'Now I've not asked what this business is,' he said, 'and very likely you'll tell me when it's a good time for me to know. But I'll make a guess the two of you have something in hand that will take all your wakefulness when we touch port, so if you heed my advice you'll go to your hammocks while I pilot the ship across this last stretch of sea.'

They did as he said. Each retired to an unoccupied chamber, where the strong wing-beats of the inn and the gentle straining and easing of its timbers soon lulled them fast asleep.

It was several hours later, though it seemed like only a few minutes, when they were woken in turn by the soft voice of Sir Politesse.

'I so regret being obliged to disturb you, and please allow me to repeat my apologies for the unfortunate events of—'

'Yes,' said Tom springing up. 'That's all right: what is it?'

'The moon,' said Sir Politesse anxiously. 'We're almost there.'

Tom headed at once for the chamber at the prow, followed by Princess Eleanor and several of the knights who were off duty. Before them lay the moon, its horizon stretching far and wide, with the moonlight rising up from it in a silvery shimmer. Jagged mountains reared darkly beyond the plains, and they saw the winding courses of rivers too, with towns clustered along them.

'The moon's a mighty mass of cheese,' murmured Princess Eleanor, and the others stared as if in a trance. The goblins, meanwhile, were more excited than ever, and the sound of their pointed slippers flapping on the floorboards could be heard all over the inn, along with frantic squeaks and occasional wolf-like howls.

'Well, someone's glad to be here,' commented the captain, and turned to find his ghostly self at his elbow.

'If someone could banish that ghost from my house, I'd give him half I own!' stormed Master Richard.

Tom smiled. 'We'll do what we can, Captain, but I won't ask you as much as that in payment.'

He looked at Tom and then at the Princess, and perhaps began to guess something of their errand. Then he turned back to the window. 'Well, then, all hands at the ready: land ahead, and there's our port!'

The Eagle turned its head and screamed, and then tilted its wings so that they slipped through the air, and the inn dropped in a sudden swoop.

'Easy, there!' cried the captain, touching the bird on its shoulder with the warming-pan, and now the Eagle soared in a long arc, always downwards, but so gently and slowly that it seemed to be playing on the high currents that danced above the surface of the moon, turning and wheeling, as eagles do when the warm air rises up from the valleys into the highest parts of the mountains, and there is nothing to do but soar and play, like whales in the deep sea.

'Where do you want us, Master Tom?' asked the captain, as the ground loomed closer every time they turned for a new sweep across the sky.

'Head for the plain,' said Tom, 'and land us near a town, if you can.'

'Right enough,' replied the seafarer, and the cold air whistled as the Eagle made shorter and shorter traverses, slowing at the end of each one to wheel round for another swoop. One by one the knights excused themselves, and stood by the rail of the gallery in a green-faced line.

Soon they had dipped below the level of the mountains which raised their broken heads in the distance, and the blank, yellow face of the plain skimmed past closer and closer below.

'It's cheese, all right,' said Master Richard, 'and

cheese of a soft and spongy kind, I'd say. We'll have to take care as we come in: I see nothing there that's fit to do for a house's foundations.'

Tom and Eleanor both felt this to be a fair comment, as they surveyed the smooth Edam Plain that sped past underneath. Here and there a stunted thorn-bush poked out of the cheese, or a quarry showed where blocks had been hewn for the neat town that stood some way off; but mostly there was no variety in the shiny, yellow surface below.

'Down we go!' shouted Master Richard, and the Eagle swooped past again, this time lower than ever. There was a thump, and gobbets of Edam flew up where the cellar steps ploughed into the ground. The inn tipped forward, and now the whole front dug itself into a firm bed of cheese. The entire mass stretched like a jelly and then flopped back, throwing them off their feet. The inn sank gently into the cheese, but then it held firm, and the Eagle was down. It gave a last screech, and folded its wings by its sides.

Tom and the Princess ran to the door, past giddy knights and excited goblins, and Eleanor was the first out on to the soft, cheesy surface of the moon.

'We're here!' she shouted, and looked all round, from the harsh mountains away on the left, to the yellow plain that stretched to the right as far as the eye could see, throbbing with a silvery light. Not far off stood the curious houses of the Moonmen, gathered alongside a cloudy stream. Above, the sky was black, and sprinkled with the brightest stars, as if it were the dead of night; but up among them shone the yellow sun, and the blue crescent of the Earth they had left behind.

'Yes,' said Tom, more soberly, 'we're here, and now the danger really begins.'

CHAPTER 11

Cheesecrown

A small party soon gathered outside the inn. Master Richard inspected the foundations, while several of the knights tottered out after him, still looking rather green after the flight. Then came the goblins, chattering and pointing excitedly. They skipped this way and that, arguing in shrill voices, and then set off at a run across the plain, their slippers flapping on the glossy surface of the cheese.

'One more mystery,' said Tom, as he watched them dwindle into the distance.

'Never mind,' said Eleanor. 'Let's go and see who's in charge of this town.'

It was a strange experience walking on something perfectly smooth and springy, which stretched for miles in every direction, and which they were more accustomed to eating on bread in very small chunks. Ahead there was a stranger sight still. The town of the Moonmen lay before them, each house fashioned of rubbery blocks of yellow Edam, and each one a more bizarre shape than the last. Some were supported on great curving arches; others had stairs running all round the outside, up and up; others again had round or diamond windows carved in their walls, as if by a sharp knife. Some were open to the stars, while others were roofed with thin slices of cheese, which hung out over the eaves.

As they wandered among the buildings, the Moonmen began to appear. They were dressed in yellow, and from under their yellow hoods and headdresses peered out round, silvery moon-faces. One by one they came up, and stood and stared, as silent as the moon itself.

Tom plucked up his courage, and called out, 'We want to see the head Moonman!'

The Moonmen fell to whispering, and their faces turned to shadow. Then a tall Moonman strode forward. He had a look of importance, and wore a Stilton cheese on his head, with a chain of water biscuits hung around his neck.

'Welcome, noble visitors!' he said in a gentle voice, and took their hands. 'I am Cheesecrown, humble head of the inoffensive cheese-people dwelling hereabouts. I judge from the manner of your coming that you are mighty folk: come to my house, and tell me your errand.'

He led them to a large building in the middle of the town. Along its front ran a portico of finely marbled pillars, all of the best Roquefort, while the mosaics inside shone with the rich shades of Blue Vinney and Red Leicester. Cheesecrown showed them into a courtyard with a fountain of buttermilk playing at its centre, and there under the stars they were feasted with all the daintiest fare the moon afforded. There was mild cheese and smelly cheese, soft cheese and hard cheese, crumbly cheese and sticky cheese; Jarlsberger dug from the mountains of the North, Esrom and Emmenthal, Cornish Yarg and Ribblesdale Goat, all washed down with fresh milk from the river.

When the meal had begun, Cheesecrown asked Tom and Eleanor why they had come. They exchanged glances, and then Princess Eleanor said confidently, 'We have come to the moon to defeat the Bold Enchanter.'

The Moonman's face glowed and then darkened, like

a moon suddenly eclipsed. 'You little know how many dangers you face,' he said at last, in a sad voice.

'Well, can you list them for us?' demanded Tom.

'The way is long and hard,' replied the Moonman. 'The Enchanter's Castle lies away on the western rim of the moon, on the edge of those lands which the Earth never sees. To get there, you must follow the River of Milk until you reach a great sea. You must travel westwards along its shore until you have crossed seven rivers, and then you will come to a great marsh of yoghurt, beset with buttery mires and swamps of treacherous cream cheese. Here the great Edam Plain comes to an end in its red domed foothills, and beyond lie the Cheddar Mountains, with the Bold Enchanter's Castle in their midst, ringed about by seven peaks.

'One of these you must scale, but each has its perils. The Parmesan Cliffs are sharp and cruel, and the round caves of the Emmenthal Valleys swarm with the wild Moonmen of the hills. Then there is the terrible Fondue Mountain, where even the Enchanter's sentinels fear to go. On its cursed slopes cheesy belches boil from the bowels of the moon, and craters of molten Gruyère lie steaming to the stars. One of these mountains you must cross, and then you will have won through to the Castle you seek.'

'And then what?' asked Princess Eleanor eagerly.

'Then you must face the Seven Sentinels. Each has seven eyes, which take it in turns to sleep, and they keep an unceasing watch over the Enchanter's Castle. But above all things you must beware of the Enchanter himself. He is a master of trickery and illusion, and can easily make bad seem good and good seem bad. Should you pay any heed to his cajolery, you will be turned to worms, and never see your homes again, as sure as cheese. Mistrust his smiles and promises, and you are a fair way to defeating him. But then you must be magicians, or the journey is in vain. Are you skilled in the magic of the moon?'

'No,' admitted Tom, 'but we have this.' And he produced the moon wand and held it for their host to see.

'Ah,' said the Moonman, his face gleaming with hope. 'Then your spells will have power. All you must do is learn to cast them, and you can practise that while you are on your journey. A moon spell is a simple thing. It has four lines, and each line has seven syllables, so that the whole magic is held in by the number twenty-eight; for in so many days the moon waxes to its full and wanes again to darkness. You must begin your spell by calling in some way on the power of the moon, or on cheese, which is its element, and then you must say what magic you wish performed. Thus you may work any wonder.'

Cheesecrown sighed deeply, and his bright face eclipsed again from one side. 'Ah, Bold Enchanter!' he wailed. 'What curses would I cast on you if I could! A wand of power, a level head, and a ready wit, these are the weapons that will work his ruin; but I fear I have none of them, nor has any other inoffensive Moonman of the Plains.'

'But we have them all three, don't we, Princess?' said Tom resolutely, and she brightened into a smile, and said, 'We do indeed, Sir Tom!'

The poor Moonman smiled too, and began to have hopes from his strange visitors from the Earth. 'Then you'll want provisions and a guide. As far as the foothills, at least: no one will dare go further than that.'

'Then we'll come back for them as soon as we've

revisited our inn—or ship,' said Tom, and they took their leave. As they walked back across the Plain from the strange-looking town, Eleanor gave Tom a nudge.

'You're not going to try any more of your foolishness about leaving me behind, are you?'

Tom smiled. 'Not any more. I've a feeling this job will take both of us.'

'Anyway, I bet I'll be at least as good as you at casting spells.'

'Very likely,' Tom admitted.

By now they were back at the inn, where a busy scene of preparation greeted them. The knights were leading their horses out from the inn yard, now paved with Edam Cheese. Sir Bivouac blew his trumpet as a call to arms, and Sir Reticule mounted up with a tremendous jangling of all the pots and pans and bags and bottles which ornamented his person.

'Forward!' cried Sir Vortigern. 'We go forth to battle giants, slay dragons, and belabour goblins, for the honour of my ancestors and the hand of the fair Princess!'

The knights let out a rousing cheer. Their banners fluttered in the gentle moon breeze, the hoofs of their horses pawed up clods of Edam, and then they were off across the Plain. As they passed, they saluted the Princess, who watched them go with a shiver.

'Come on,' she said to Tom, 'before they have the chance to do anything heroic.'

Inside, they found Master Richard sitting alone, and Princess Eleanor told him quickly of their mission.

'I see you're set on it,' he said, 'so I shan't make any argument. I'll wait your return and mind the Eagle. It's just me and the ghost aboard, now the knights have left: even the goblins have jumped ship. Well, there's little I can do, but here's something that might be of use.' He handed them a pair of bottles. 'This one's moonshine, such as sent the knights into such a howling dwam. This other's a bottle of my best ale: it might be a comfort in those hard mountains off yonder. And good luck to you both.'

They thanked him, and set off back to the town, leaving the innkeeper standing under the carved eagle, now asleep with its oaken head tucked under a wooden wing.

The Moonmen turned out in great numbers as Tom and Eleanor arrived, and stared and stared, but none of them dared to cheer. The pair soon recognized the Stilton headdress of Cheesecrown coming towards them through the crowd. At that moment, Eleanor suddenly broke away from Tom's side. She had seen a sort of moonish bookshop down a side-street, and had had an idea. When she rejoined him, she was wearing a mysterious smile, and Cheesecrown was handing Tom a pair of bulging haversacks.

'My friends,' he said, 'here I have packed for your journey some of the choicest dainties from my larder. And now let me present the inoffensive Chompjaw, a Moonman well versed in the moonography of all the rivers and seas of our Edam Plain. He will guide you as far as the foothills, but beyond there, alas, we can do no more.'

Tom and Eleanor thanked Cheesecrown heartily for his welcome and his advice, and set off down the river with Chompjaw. The silent, moon-faced stares of the cheese-people followed them out of sight, and the stark, yellow mountains rose ahead.

CHAPTER 12

Into the Mountains

Their way led them along the winding River of Milk, which flowed with a quiet babble along a furrow in the surface of the Plain. The cheese stretched on and on, yielding slightly under their feet, and covered in tiny drops of oil that had oozed up with the heat of the sun.

'I don't think I'll ever eat cheese again,' said Princess Eleanor in distaste, after they had been walking for some time.

'I think you will,' said Tom, 'because we've nothing else for lunch or supper.'

Eleanor heaved a deep sigh. A little while later she said, 'I've been thinking, Tom, about a funny thing that happened at home, when our silly jester turned Lady Clara into a duck by mistake.'

'What's that?' asked Tom in surprise.

'You see, he cast a moon spell without knowing it. It went,

> 'By the mighty magic pow'rs
> making goblins run amuck—'

'Yes yes,' Tom interrupted. 'I'm sure you're right, but I don't want to find myself turned into a duck so soon in the expedition.'

Eleanor laughed playfully. 'You're so unreasonable! Cheesecrown told us we ought to practise our spells.'

'Not on each other,' objected Tom.

'Who better to practise on?' demanded the Princess,

as Chompjaw eyed her fearfully from under his yellow hood, and quickened his pace.

'How about this one:

> 'By the moonlit midnight hour,
> by the silent misty night;
> coat the miller's boy in flour,
> make him look a perfect fright!'

As she finished speaking, a cloud of flour sprang out of Tom's clothing, and he burst into a fit of coughing. Princess Eleanor clapped her hands in glee, and then thumped Tom on the back.

'I'm sorry, Tom! Are you all right?'

'Oh, fine,' wheezed Tom. 'With a bit of luck I'll look like a ghost and frighten the enemy out of their skins.'

'Doubtful,' said the Princess critically. 'Don't forget some of the enemy probably *are* ghosts; and besides, you look more like a goblin.'

'The same to you,' retorted Tom. 'You're as full of pranks as one, anyway.'

After that, they went on making up spells to pass the time, while they trudged wearily on beside the milky river. Now and then they passed a small settlement of Moonmen, and sometimes they saw openings in the ground where the cheese-people mined for their food. Once they passed a line of silent miners setting off with cocktail-sticks over their shoulders, and later on they saw chunks of blue and yellow Stilton stuck on poles in the sun to dry.

At last, a shimmer of white was visible in the distance ahead, and the great Sea of Milk came gradually into sight. Soon they could hear it sighing against its shores, where the wind had whipped up a foam of great white bubbles, and the air was sweet with its smell.

'Sea of Milk,' said their guide briefly, his moon-face shining from deep inside its hood, and then he led them on along the shore, with the milky froth seething and crackling on their right and the yellow, greasy plain stretching off to their left. They had not been walking long when they came to the second river, a meandering stream of sour milk, with red baby Edams lying in its bed like nuggets. They crossed by a sweeping bridge of Edam blocks, and soon came to the third. This river was of double cream, surging sluggishly past sturdy Gouda stepping-cheeses.

They had left the last of the villages behind now, and came to a region of scattered woods. Bare twigs and sticks rose all round, with giant stuffed olives and pickled onions stuck on them.

'Good to eat,' said Chompjaw, with another of his secret smiles. Tom and Eleanor decided to take the hint, and unpacked some of their food. Chompjaw's face brightened; he very rarely saw such exotic cheeses as his chief had stored away in his larder. The other two, however, were rather less enthusiastic.

'You'd think,' said the Princess, 'that after walking on cheese all day, we might have had a change from it for lunch.'

Still, the cheeses were varied and good, and after Tom discovered another tree with jars of chutney growing on it, the feast was complete.

They set off again. The jagged tops of the Cheddar Mountains now rose up close ahead, with the foothills in front of them, and soon they came to three more rivers. All were rushing mountain streams, and they forded them easily on beds of Parmesan pebbles which had been washed down from the hills. The first seemed to be buttermilk, the second single cream. The third was thin and watery, with small white lumps carried down on the swift current.

'Curds and whey,' explained Chompjaw, looking up at the Mountains in fear. 'Sixth river!' A shadow spread over his face, and he hurried on, bending low and muttering to himself.

There were already signs that the Edam Plain was coming to an end. Instead of the smooth, yellow surface of cheese stretching unbroken in every direction, here there were rifts and wedges, and rounded hummocks where the cheese showed its red waxy rind. As they skirted one of these glossy, red humps, they came to the seventh and last river, and Chompjaw stopped. He seemed more frightened than ever.

'Seventh river,' he whispered. 'Béchamel, hot and creamy. Past here the country's wild! Wild, and unlucky!' He stared into both their faces, his own brightening and dimming with emotion.

'Well,' said the Princess, trying not to catch the Moonman's fear, 'you promised to take us at least as far as the end of the Yoghurt Marsh, and then you can go back if you want to.'

Chompjaw turned away, nestling his round face down inside his hood, and muttered about the madness of the Earth-people. Then he scrambled down the bank and cleared the seventh river, jumping from one slippery gobbet of rind to another. The other two followed, pausing to taste the hot, rich sauce that flowed down from the hills.

'Hot springs,' explained Chompjaw. 'Very unlucky. Come on!' Beyond the river, the ground stretched out level in a succession of greasy pools and sluggish milky streams. Chompjaw led them on in silence by a roundabout route, and they were very careful to follow exactly in his footsteps. Off on either side there were round pits, filled to the brim with soft white lumps of cottage cheese, while all around stretched the greenish, quivering surface of the yoghurt, which looked firm, but would have been more treacherous than quicksand to any who tried to walk on it. In some places the ground was more solid, and they walked over a small rise of Edam, with muddy ruts of butter gathered at its edges where the marsh resumed. They trudged along stoutly, daubed up to the knees with mire, resting only once in a grove of giant grapes stuck on sticks; but the wide eyes and muttering of the Moonman prevented any conversation.

At last they reached the end of the marsh, where the great red domes of the Edam Foothills began. They turned and thanked their guide, who replied with a stare of horror.

'Don't go on!' he pleaded. 'Come back with me, where the luck's better! Don't go on!'

'You go back,' said Tom. 'No one's pressing you to go any further.'

The Moonman gave them a last bright stare, then turned and ran hopping back over the marsh, until very soon they could hear him splashing through the river of hot sauce and panting up the bank on the other side.

'And now we're alone,' said Tom, turning to look at the glossy red hills ahead, shining against the black, starry sky.

'So much the better,' said the Princess briskly, taking Tom's arm. 'I can't bear people who moan. Let's see what these hills are like!'

Tom cast a spell to clean the butter and mire from their clothes, and they set off along a narrow path of level cheese that led between the waxy domes of Edam rind.

They could sense the closeness of danger. The view down the avenues that wound between the great red cheeses shifted constantly, and they kept glancing around, every moment expecting some ambush in the silent, uncanny maze.

They pressed on at random deeper into the hills, until at last the way between the cheeses became so narrow that they were forced to climb up their slippery sides. Tom cut out flaps of rind with his knife for footholds, and so they climbed gingerly on. Soon the Edam Foothills lay behind, like a froth of red bubbles, and ahead stretched the true Mountains, receding upwards in a mass of jagged blocks and ledges.

'Now what?' asked the Princess brightly.

'As if it isn't obvious,' Tom replied with a smile. 'We climb the Mountains.'

A jumble of different cheeses lay ahead. In places there were hard, oily outcrops of Parmesan, which they skirted round; sometimes they found themselves walking gingerly up a great block of Gouda set at a steep slant, and sometimes they scrambled over crags of crumbly Cheddar, the true native cheese of the Mountains; but always they climbed higher and higher, with silence all around and the stars above, and never a sign of a Moonman.

They came at last to a plateau whose smooth surface was dotted with boulders of many kinds, left behind when the great ice-caps of frozen yoghurt and ice cream had retreated to the northern parts of the moon. The going here was easier, and Princess Eleanor collapsed beside a huge chunk of Red Leicester.

'I'm so tired,' she complained; 'and so thirsty, too. Don't you think it's strange, the way the sun's so hot, while the sky's all black and starry?'

'I think a lot of things are strange,' said Tom, sitting down beside her, with a glance around at the yellow plateau with its towering boulders, and the blue sliver of the crescent Earth hanging low in the eastern sky.

'If only there were something to drink,' added Eleanor, and then her eye strayed to a pool of liquid lying not far from their boulder, and she jumped up eagerly. 'Look! It's water!'

'I don't believe it,' said Tom from the ground. 'There's nothing on the moon but butter and milk and cheese and cream.'

'But there is,' insisted the Princess, who had knelt by the pool, and whose cupped hands were dripping with a cool, silvery fluid.

Tom looked again, and then started suddenly. 'Stop! Don't drink!'

'But why not?' demanded the Princess rather crossly, lowering her hands into the gleaming pool and cupping them afresh.

'Don't you see? That's not real water. It's moonshine.'

Eleanor let the bright drops run out through her fingers. 'I suppose you're right,' she admitted. 'But I'm so fed up with milk! One day I'll have a house beside a stream, and I'll just listen to it babble day and night, and drink from it whenever I want, and never have any milk or cheese ever again!'

'But in the meantime,' said Tom, passing her the flask which Cheesecrown had given them, 'milk is what we've got, and a small amount of ale, but we may be glad of that later.'

Princess Eleanor took the flask and drank. 'I don't see why you couldn't have let me *try* the moonshine at least,' she said. 'If I *had* turned into a moonsick loon you could always have cured me with your magic stone, and I do so wonder what it tastes like.'

'Please, Princess. We mustn't take risks, even if— What was that?'

They tensed. From the other side of the boulder, they could hear the tramp of many feet, and the faint sound of singing. They crept carefully round until they caught sight of a band of Moonmen, filing up from the plain below, and the sight and sound of them struck Tom and Eleanor with dread.

Their leader was whirling a gleaming steel cheese-knife in the air, and all of the others were armed to the teeth, either with walnut-headed clubs or sharpened cocktail-spears. They were dressed in rags and patches of grey and brown, so that in the shadows of the boulders they seemed to disappear. Over their shoulders they were carrying great lumps of Stilton mounted on cocktail-sticks.

'The wild men of the Mountains,' Tom whispered. 'They've been down to raid the Lowlanders.'

'Quiet!' Eleanor whispered, and they crouched out of sight while the Moonmen passed, roaring with laughter about the shock they'd given to the peaceful Plain-dwellers. At last the column moved out of sight, and their din vanished after them.

Princess Eleanor was leaning against the boulder, feeling shaken.

'I don't want them to catch us, Tom,' she said.

'They won't,' Tom assured her. 'But you're not frightened, are you? Not the plucky Princess?'

'No,' Eleanor replied, 'but there was something so wild about them. I'm beginning to see why Chompjaw was so much afraid of these hills.'

'Well, let's press on. We'll be clear of the Mountains

soon, and then there's only the Enchanter to worry about.'

They set off again uphill, veering away from the direction the Moonmen had taken. Ahead the Mountains rose up to the stars in dizzying sweeps, while sun and Earth shone low in the sky behind.

'I think that means we're nearing the western rim of the moon,' said Princess Eleanor. 'Since the moon is full, you see, the sun and the Earth are in the same part of the sky: the Earth's between the two, and that's why it only looks like a tiny crescent.'

'I don't see that,' said Tom, as they entered the mouth of a valley leading deeper into the Mountains.

The Princess sighed. 'You're so slow! If only I could show you on the astrolabe that's kept in the Castle Library, you'd soon see what I mean.'

'Millers' sons don't get much schooling in astronomy as a rule,' pointed out Tom.

'I think it's a scandal. When we get back, I'll pester my father until he sets up a special academy so that all the millers' sons in the Kingdom can learn about the rotation of the Earth and not be so horribly ignorant all the time.'

By now they had gone a good way up the valley. Rows of curling walnut crags lined the slopes above them, and the cheese here was white and shiny, and pitted with hollow depressions. Here and there they could see the dark openings of rounded caves.

Princess Eleanor let out a gasp. 'Oh, Tom! Don't you remember what Cheesecrown said about the round caves of the Emmenthal Valleys?'

Tom stopped in alarm, but before he could reply, the Princess had let out a shrill shriek, and disappeared in front of his eyes.

114

'Princess!' he shouted, and at the same moment he heard harsh voices, and Moonmen began to pour from the openings.

'I'm all right!' came a muffled voice from below his feet. Tom crouched down, and saw that the Princess had fallen into a round underground cavern, all but hidden by a thin flap of rubbery cheese.

'Pull me up!' she called. Tom reached his arm down the hole, his eyes fixed anxiously on the Moonmen. They were gathering in large numbers, and now they let out cruel whoops and rushed down on him, waving their walnut war-hammers over their heads.

'What is it?' called out Princess Eleanor, imprisoned in the bubble-shaped chamber, with only Tom's hand waving uncertainly through the narrow hole above her head.

'The Moonmen. I'll have to do something.' He snatched back his arm and racked his brains for a spell or a plan, while the Princess stamped with frustration. The hillmen were only a few steps away, when Tom began to speak.

> 'By the Moon on which we stand,
> by its cliffs of Cheddar cheese;
> may the bludgeons in your hand . . . '

The clubs were poised to come down on his skull, and Tom shrieked:

> ' . . . turn to pickled anchovies!'

The fierce walnut hammers vanished, and the Moonmen stopped to stare in horror at their hands, suddenly clutching messy bits of fish. In a moment, though, their rage returned. They pelted Tom with the anchovies, and prepared to spring on him with their bare hands.

Meanwhile, from within her cheesy cell, Princess Eleanor heard the cries of the wild Moonmen above, and felt the quivering of the cheese around her as they ran madly on. She tried in vain to jump up and catch hold of the lip of the pit, and fell back on the rounded floor of Emmenthal with a cry of anger. Then she frowned and tried to concentrate.

The Moonmen had laid rough hands on Tom, and were already uttering terrible threats and shaking their fists in his face, when they heard a rhythmic chant which seemed to come from somewhere under their feet. They stopped to listen, disturbed and entranced.

> 'Moonlit midnight's magic soul,
> pools of moonshine, cliffs of cheese;
> may I, risen from this hole,
> strike with dread my enemies!'

With the last words of the spell, Princess Eleanor rose from the pit as if carried up on a platform, and stood in the midst of the Moonmen. Tom turned to look, expecting them to seize her as well. But the wild Moonmen backed slowly away, and when Eleanor gave Tom a smile, the hillmen began to babble and point, and then they turned and fled, stretching their arms out and weeping with fear.

'What on earth did you do to them?' demanded Tom.

'You should say "what on moon", not "what on earth". You're forgetting where you are! I've no idea what I did. They must have thought I was some awful ogre about to gobble them up. Anyway, let's get out of this dangerous valley before they get over their shock.'

They headed for the steep valley sides, Tom picking anchovies off himself as they went.

'You silly thing!' Eleanor exclaimed. 'What made you cast a spell like that?'

'It was all I could think of. Yours did the trick, though: I said you were a handy lass!'

'Flatterer!' replied the Princess. 'Race you to that big walnut, then!' She set off at a run, and Tom followed. The smooth slope got steeper and steeper as they neared the top, but with a good run-up they managed to grab on to its edge without slipping back, and sat panting between the great bluffs of shiny walnut that poked up from the surface of the cheese all along the lip of the great valley.

From here they could look back on the drab Edam Plain, now far below them to the east, while ahead a wide panorama of mountains had opened up, sweeping in a circuit from left to right as far as they could see. Furthest off they saw a chain of pointed peaks, suggesting some sort of smelly goat-cheese; then the towering, jagged mass of the Parmesan Mountain, and the gentler Emmenthal Valleys, teeming, as they knew, with the bloodthirsty men of the hills. To their right lay the Fondue Mountain, where the mighty cones of bubbling volcanoes thrust their tops among the stars. Savoury steam issued from their vents, yellow in the low light of the sun, and even at a distance they could hear the echoing gurgles and hollow belches made by seething underground channels of molten cheese.

'Well?' said Tom.

'The Fondue Mountain it is,' said the Princess. 'The Moonmen will never dare follow us up that.'

They set off once more, over a strange landscape dotted with towering, wedge-shaped boulders, dazzling with silver on one side, deeply shadowed on the other. These, they soon saw, were soft cheese segments of many flavours, tomato, mushroom, and garlic, all wrapped in silver foil and bearing a brightly printed paper label, recording the cheese's flavour and exact fat content.

It was a hard climb up to the great ridge in front of them, with volcanoes rumbling and groaning on either side. The ground was warm under their feet; sometimes it trembled with a dull roar that resounded from the many pores and crannies which riddled the Mountain. From one cave they passed, smoke curled as from the mouth of a dragon, while another bubbled with some rich cheese sauce, redolent of white wine and herbs. A third bellowed as if a bull were trapped inside, and another murmured on and on like a human voice, lamenting its lot to the lonely mountains, never pausing, or caring if anyone heard.

As they reached the high pass on the very crest of the ridge, clouds of sweet-smelling steam blew across, blotting the path from sight. They groped their way forward, and then the breeze shifted, and just ahead they saw a great round pit of bubbling, seething cheese, kept a-simmer by the fires that burned in the heart of the moon. Lumps of smoked cheese had formed beside the reeking vents, and the broken cheese-blocks of the mountain were soft and shiny where they had begun to melt in the heat. By the side of the Fondue Volcano there stood a grove of white croutons stuck on long steel forks, as if the whole mountain had been devised by some giant for his supper-table.

The smell made them hungry, but there was something depressing in the sight too, and they were glad to hurry away from that gigantic scene of food dominating man. They ran past the crater, bathed in its fragrant steam, which first enveloped them in a cloud of

scalding vapour, and then blew past, leaving them damp
and shivering. They were only just short of the ridge
now, and could look down into several of the gaping
pools of cheese. They dodged behind a glistening block
of warm Cheddar just in time to shield themselves from
a shower of boiling milk that fell from a nearby geyser,
and hurried on again up to the top of the slope.

Then, very weary, they reached the ridge and could
look out over the country beyond. Ahead stretched the
broad and broken plateau of the Cheddar Mountains,
lying within its chain of seven peaks, and in its centre,
towering up from a great hard crag of rind, stood the
Castle of the Bold Enchanter of the Moon. The
Mountains cast long shadows across the wilderness that
lay at their feet, but the Castle stood proud in the light
of the sun, on the very western brink of the part of the
moon seen from Earth. Beyond, all was darkness, and
that yellow fortress rode like a stately galley in a sea of
shadows, the polished blocks of its walls catching the
sun and shining out like a beacon. Steam from its
boiling moat rose about it in wisps, and the light of the
stars cast a pale glow over the darkened land round
about, where not a tree or river was anywhere to be
seen.

Eleanor shuddered, and Tom frowned, and then they
set off down the slope to seek out the Bold Enchanter.

CHAPTER 13

In the Enchanter's Castle

Beyond the high pass, they at once found themselves in deep shadow. Clefts and hollows were only dimly visible as darker patches in the feeble starlight, and many a time they came close to stumbling over some unseen edge. After a time they came to more level ground, with the glowing yellow form of the Enchanter's Castle perched on its peak ahead of them like a great lamp set above a dark floor.

They moved on in silence, absorbed in thoughts of what was to come, and looking carefully all round for signs of danger. Soon they discovered they were no longer alone. A grey flight of ghosts startled them first, blowing coldly past in tatters, the land beyond showing through their hollow eyes. They flew noiselessly by, and soon could be seen circling the bright Castle like moths against a flame.

Then, not long afterwards, they dodged into a stunted grove of celery sticks and hid while a troop of Moonmen passed. They marched stiffly off, neither tame and gentle as the Lowlanders, nor wild and free-spirited like the men of the hills, and Tom and Eleanor concluded that they were under the Enchanter's spell, and had been conjured by him to work some wicked deed.

'Tom,' said Eleanor, giving him a nudge as they emerged from the celery, 'what are we going to do?'

'You always ask me that just when I don't know,' replied Tom. 'Well, we'll have to get into the Castle somehow: that's the first thing.'

They were very close now. A well-trodden path led up past hard crags of extra-mature Cheddar to the very gate of the Castle, where the moat bubbled and steamed, and the smooth walls of the keep rose sheer to the stars. A flurry of what looked like dead leaves at their feet made them jump, and a swarm of dark shapes started up and swirled chattering round them like torn pieces of paper on the wind, with eyes and hands. The Princess gave a scream and beat them away, and they flew off in a line towards the Castle.

'What was that?' exclaimed Tom in dismay.

'I don't care what it was!' retorted the Princess. 'I don't want it, and I didn't ask for it, and it can go away!'

'Well, look. Let's get nearer the Castle and see if we can think of a plan.'

They advanced warily, until they were hidden behind a crag immediately below the drawbridge. From beyond their hiding place the smell of melted cheese once again drifted down on them.

'A fondue moat ten fathoms deep,' quoted Princess Eleanor.

'And sentinels who never sleep,' added Tom.

At that moment, they heard a grinding of wheels and chains, and the great drawbridge, fashioned of sturdy planks of cheese, was slowly lowered. They waited breathless. It came to rest beside their crag with a thump, and a lumbering creature strode out from the Castle, its feet echoing loudly on the drawbridge. They peeped round to see a giant advancing towards them, coloured to match the cheese of the Mountains.

Tom felt horribly watched, and then he realized why. Between the two eyes which it had in the usual place, there was a third in its forehead, and in the middle of each cheek was one eye more, while from the palms of its hands stared a sixth eye and a seventh. Eleanor buried her face in her hands, and the giant blinked first here and then there, and cast its eyes about every way at once, as if scanning for their hiding place.

They sank down behind their crag, but the Sentinel fixed its seven eyes on the spot, and came round the bend in the path until it was facing them.

'Honoured guests,' said the giant in a dry, rumbling voice, 'I am instructed by the Enchanter to make you welcome. If you will follow me, I shall take you to him, for he is most anxious to meet you.' It bowed low, and as it did so, the eye in its forehead stared straight through them. Then it turned its back and walked back over the drawbridge, trusting them to follow.

'Well?' whispered the Princess.

'We go in,' replied Tom, and they scurried out and caught up with their guide. As they reached the path, the glare of the distant eastern sun fell full on them, and its sudden brilliance made them feel more spied on than ever. They passed over the steaming moat and under the great gatehouse, with its mighty cheesen gates and strong hinges, wrought by smiths of the toughest Parmesan. Beyond, a pair of Sentinels stood with great steel halberds, their ends bent back in a double point like a cheese-knife. The Sentinels bowed low with grave smiles, and they passed on into a courtyard.

'It's just like my dream,' whispered Princess Eleanor to Tom. He looked at her enquiringly, but there was no time to talk as the giant led them on to a flight of steps at the far end of the courtyard. There another pair of Sentinels met them, and greeted them with the same bows and smiles. Eleanor's heart was beating fast. Every moment she expected their welcome to come to an end, the trumpet to be blown, and goblin guards to pour down on them from every side.

The quiet, smiling reception continued, however, and soon they were standing at a great door at the end of a long passage, where the final pair of Sentinels smiled and bowed low, the single eyes on their foreheads again probing them without expression. Their guide went before them through the door, and then returned and beckoned them on. They followed; Tom was practising his spells, and made sure the wand and the three magic stones were handy for use, but at the sight before them they stopped in dismay.

The room they had entered was wallpapered with a faded pattern of pinkish roses; its furniture was plain and rather rickety, and at a table facing the window sat a hunched old man with his back to them. As they entered he turned in his chair to look at them. He had a bald head with tufts of grey hair about the ears, and a small pair of spectacles sat on his large nose. His look was mild and fretful, and he regarded them with something of a harassed air, as if he were afraid of what his visitors might do to him. At his elbow was a cracked teacup with a biscuit perched on the saucer, and he seemed to have just been reading from a small book, in which he kept his place with one finger.

'Are . . . are you the Enchanter?' asked Princess Eleanor in amazement.

'I am,' replied the old man mildly. 'And I think I remember seeing you once before, my dear, perhaps in a dream?'

'I did dream about you,' replied Eleanor in confusion, 'but you didn't look at all the way you do now.'

'Ah, my dear,' answered the Enchanter with a thin smile, 'dreams can be very deceptive, you know. And I have such malicious enemies who slander one most dreadfully.' The corners of his mouth drooped, and he looked more fretful than ever.

Tom was all in a fog; he had released his grip on the magic stones and was staring at the old man in puzzlement. Was he really not such a villain as they had thought? One idea came back to him, that they must recover the missing wand, and if the Enchanter was as reasonable as he looked, that oughtn't to be difficult.

'We don't want to waste too much of your time,' Tom began, while their host turned a worried eye on him, 'so I'll tell you why we've come. The Lady of the Woods, who lives on Earth, has lost her wand, and she thinks that you may have it: and we would like to take it back to her, if so.' Tom's heart thumped in his chest as the Enchanter went on staring at him sadly, as if waiting for him to take back what he had said.

'Ah,' said the old man at last, 'yes, the famous Lady of the Woods and her wand. I shan't deny I've got it: I hate falsehood and everything that resembles it. Yes, I have her wand.'

'And can we have it?' pursued Tom.

'No,' replied the Enchanter carelessly.

'But it's her property,' Tom insisted, beginning to be irritated.

'You mean it *was* her property,' the Enchanter corrected him. 'The Lady of the Woods took it from a tree when she cut it, and now I've taken it from her. Property is theft, my dear young man.' And the Enchanter smiled on Tom pityingly.

'No,' replied Tom hotly. '*Theft* is theft: property is property. And if you don't give it to us, we'll take it. It's just that simple.'

'Now, now, now,' said the Enchanter, raising his

white eyebrows. 'You are a very aggressive young man, and I think we should all think carefully before taking any steps. But before we do that, have the two of you considered the company you're keeping?'

He looked at Tom and Eleanor meaningfully, with several grave nods, and Tom looked to the companion by his side. His eyes opened wide, and instead of the kind and lively Princess he knew, he saw a cold and haughty figure, a tall icicle of a Princess, whose chin tilted above his head in high disdain, and whose nostrils flared with contempt. Her hand was extended to the old man, as if she thought him more her equal, and she smiled in the Enchanter's direction with a look of frosty courtesy.

Tom was cut to the quick by her scorn, and felt all at once very lonely. Then anger flamed up in him, and he knew that Eleanor could never look at him in the way he had just seen. He reached for the emerald, which burned in his hand, and at once he saw before him the old Princess, always gentle and never haughty or proud except in fun. She looked as much alone and adrift as he had felt only a moment before, and without thinking he tossed her the stone.

Princess Eleanor, meanwhile, had been saddened to her very soul to see the poor, abject creature at her side. The miller's boy was dressed in rags; his shoulders drooped and his head hung forward awkwardly as he begged on his knees to the Enchanter for mercy. Her hero, her Tom who was kind and brave, was now a cowardly beggar at the tyrant's feet. She flared with angry disbelief, and at the same moment the emerald flew through the air and she caught it, and the illusion was gone.

'It's all a lie!' shouted Tom, and the whole room

underwent a change. The roses on the wallpaper uncoiled themselves into snakes and slithered down off the wall, leaving it bare and bleak; the teacup turned into a proud silver goblet and the biscuit hopped off as a warty toad. The old man's humble chair swelled to a gaudy throne with armrests carved as screaming mandrakes, while dark bats' wings shot from its back, and the little book grew to a heavy volume of enchantments. While everything around him changed and grew or shrank, the old man himself shook off all signs of weakness, and stood before them tall and grim and young. His shabby clothes swelled into a great cloak, his hair darkened and grew over his brow, and his nose shrank to a sharp line.

'I'll make you sorry!' hissed the Enchanter. 'I'll make you eat your insults and repent your boldness! Guards! Sentinels! Ghosts and spectres! Imps and impets! Come to me, my minions, and avenge my wrongs!'

Trumpets brayed from every part of the Castle, and sounds of running, shouting, groaning, and shrieking could be heard coming in a confused din from above, below, and around. Tom drew out his wand as the doors were thrown open, and the Enchanter's creatures poured into the room. At their head strode the tall Sentinels, and behind swarmed the goblins, cheese-knife swords and walnut maces gripped and ready.

Eleanor ran over to Tom, but at that moment a hatch opened in the floor and he was gone, while a Sentinel strode forward and seized her by the scruff of the neck.

'To the dungeons with her!' commanded the Enchanter, as the goblins milled about the room in disorder, looking down the hole and into everywhere, and clattering their weapons against their shields with warlike whoops.

'Find her friend too,' hissed the Enchanter to another

of the Sentinels. 'He offends me, and has a dangerous look. And call away these nasty goblins!'

'It will be done, Master,' rasped the Sentinel with a bow, while the first Sentinel lifted Eleanor from the ground, tucked her under one arm, and bore her off, kicking and struggling and shouting, towards the lower regions of the Castle.

CHAPTER 14

The Lodestone

Princess Eleanor was carried along passage after passage and down stair after stair, all the time jolted roughly under the giant's arm. It was hot in those narrow corridors; the stale, sickly smell of melted cheese hung in the air, and clung to the giant's body as if it were itself made of cheese, and in danger of melting.

'Put me down!' Eleanor shouted, trying to kick free.

'I'll do that soon enough,' rumbled the Sentinel, as they entered a wide, dimly lit hall. It unlocked a great door made of dirty strips of cheese fastened across each other many times with hard Parmesan rivets. 'Here we are,' went on the giant. 'This is your home, until the Enchanter decides what to turn you into, and I think you'll find it's something very nasty. In the meantime, see if you can make friends with the Horrible Hobgoblin.'

The creature threw her down roughly on the hard floor of the cell and swung shut the mighty door, which it locked with seven keys. Eleanor sat and shouted with vexation, and then thought of the giant's last words, and looked fearfully about her dungeon. A fitful ray of light fell from a high window, picking out the litter of grated cheese which lay scattered over the floor instead of straw. The corners of the cell were in darkness, and in one of them Eleanor saw a shadow which moved. She drew in her breath in alarm, but a hoarse, cracked voice from the corner spoke to reassure her.

'Don't be disturbed,' it said, and it sounded like the

dry creak of shoes or bellows that have gone much too long unoiled. 'I pity your distress, and would relieve it if I could; but alas, I have fallen from my high estate, and am powerless.'

'And who are you?' asked the Princess, still uneasy.

'I,' said the voice, 'am the Prince of Hobgoblins.' And a dry and wrinkled creature crept out of the corner into the light. Its arms and legs were withered to spindles, and its large and ugly face was pinched and shiny like parched leather. Eleanor let out a gasp, and took out the goblin coin which Tom had given her. The face was the same, even down to the three pimples which ornamented it.

'King of Pranks and Lord of Mischief,' she read, and the Prince of Hobgoblins darted forward towards the glint of the gold.

'One of my own coins!' rasped the goblin, and collapsed again into the cheese shavings. It sat for a time in silence, shaken by shudders.

'Forgive me,' it said at last. 'It was the thought of the old days of my prosperity that made me weep, and I can only weep inside. My tears have been dried up by seven thirsty years in this dungeon. The Enchanter would have had me drink his moonshine: then, when I had lost my wits and become a moonsick loon, he would have bound me to his service, as he has done so many of my former subjects. Every day the jailer sets down a jug of moonshine and a chunk of cheese, and every day I eat the cheese and leave the jug. For seven years I have drunk nothing, and every day sees me drier and more shrivelled than the last. But I shall never give in.' The goblin's rasping voice shrank to a whisper and trailed into silence.

Princess Eleanor felt very sorry for the Hobgoblin,

and tried to cheer it up by telling her own story, and assuring it that help was probably very near.

'Tom always looks after me,' she said confidently. 'Except sometimes,' she added on reflection, 'when I look after Tom. Come to think of it, he might be needing me now, and perhaps we ought to escape. Let's see: do you have any magic powers, trapdoors, secret passages, or anything else of that sort?'

'No,' confessed the goblin Prince with a hissing sigh, 'or I would have used them.'

'True,' said the Princess, and sighed as well.

Just then, they heard the stamp of the giant Sentinel outside the cell door, singing and talking to itself.

'Now, how does it go?' rumbled the giant.

> 'Honest Jack and simple Jane
> in happiness did dwell,
> tumtumtytum-tumtumtytum—
> and something something well,

'Or "fell"? Or was it "smell"?' The giant roared and kicked a stool across the room. 'Oh, *why* can't I remember? Why am I cursed with such a bad memory?'

Princess Eleanor was listening keenly at the door, and then her face broke into a bright smile.

'The Book of Ballads!' She felt in the pouch at her side, and triumphantly drew out a book. She had promised Tom that she would replace the book of ballads that Prattlebox had stolen, and when she caught sight of a bookseller's shop in the town of the Moonmen the idea had come back to her. Then they had set off on their journey, and she had forgotten all about it until that moment. Now she leafed quickly through its pages, and sang in a clear voice:

'Honest Jack and simple Jane
  in happiness did dwell,
until one dark and doomsome day
  when wicked woe befell.'

The jailer stopped its pacing and muttering out of
words that rhyme with 'dwell', and there was silence on
the other side of the door. Princess Eleanor sang the
verse again. There was a gasp, and the giant strode up
close to the mighty door, sighing in ecstasy.

'For years I've been trying to remember how that
went,' it moaned. 'But there's more—dare I hope? Do
you know how it goes on?'

'Why yes,' said Eleanor. 'I do, as a matter of fact.'

'Oh please sing me it!' begged the giant. 'Please,
please, please!'

'It's very long,' she replied doubtfully. 'Why don't I
find a nice short one? Let me see, here's one: it's
called "Simon Simple".'

'Oh, Simon Simple!' bellowed the Sentinel, shaking
the cheesy floor as it bounded up and down. 'Give me
Simon Simple, oh, Simon Simple! Yes!'

'Simon Simple had a pimple
  halfway down his nose,' Eleanor began,
and then broke off.

'Oh, but this is *most* unsuitable! I can't sing you this!
It's not the sort of thing a nice, well-brought-up giant
ought to hear at all.'

'But I'm not a nice well-brought-up giant,' wailed the
giant. 'I'm a coarse and brutal one! And I demand—I
implore you to sing it! I'll do anything!'

'Oh?' queried the Princess. 'Well, if you were to let
me and my friend go . . .'

131

'Oh, I couldn't do that,' said the giant hastily. 'The Enchanter would never forgive me, and I'd come to a grisly end.'

'Oh, well,' replied the Princess offhand, 'that's a shame, because I think then I'll have to feed the book to the Hobgoblin, who's very hungry, and has been eyeing it for some time. Of course if you *could* have seen your way to letting us out, I would have let you keep the book for your very own, for ever and ever, and there's all sorts more in it besides those two: it's even got ''The Tender-Hearted Octopus'' . . . '

She let her voice die away in an unconcerned tone, and a second later there was the thump of cheesy keys in cheesen locks, repeated seven times, and the mighty door swung open. Eleanor skipped out, followed by the spindly, shrivelled goblin, and when they were beyond the reach of the Sentinel's powerful arms, she tossed it the Book of Ballads. Then she led the Prince of Hobgoblins quickly off along the passage. She needn't have worried about being pursued, for the giant Sentinel was now deaf to all the world, eating up the book with all seven eyes, and chuckling and weeping by turns over the ballads it had yearned for so long.

At that moment, in another part of the Enchanter's Castle, Tom was wandering through a maze of dim, dank corridors. The goblin guards had so far not managed to catch up with him. Several times he had hidden against the wall as they passed by at the end of some nearby passage, but the truth was that they were untrained troops, and were as lost as he was.

Tom had been shaken by his brush with the Enchanter's illusions, and now that he had lost the Princess his mind was in a daze, and he kept dwelling on all the terrible things which might be happening to her. In the end he saw he was getting nowhere by his wanderings, so he made himself sit down and think. He took out the three stones the Lady of the Woods had given him, the golden topaz shot with silver rays, the dull blue-grey lodestone, and the emerald of tropical green. He put the others away and laid the lodestone in the palm of his hand, remembering the Lady's words: the stone would be drawn to the thing he desired most. His duty was clear: he must confront the Enchanter and defeat him.

He closed his fist over the stone, and at once was pulled to his feet by its iron grip. Along one passage and down the next the lodestone drew him, faster and always faster, until he had to run to keep up. Then he heard a rasping voice and the sound of footsteps from around a bend, and he braced himself for a meeting with his enemy. He was dragged round the corner nearly off his feet, and cannoned straight into Princess Eleanor. They fell sprawling on the ground, and Tom's arm lay stretched out, the lodestone in his fist now heavy and lifeless.

'Tom!' shouted the Princess in delight, sitting up.

Tom blinked in surprise, and then caught sight of Princess Eleanor's companion. 'Look out!' he shouted. 'It's a goblin!'

'Oh, this is my friend, the Prince of Hobgoblins,' explained Eleanor. 'Prince, this is my champion, Tom: the one I was telling you about.'

Tom blushed as he took the creature's leathery paw with a bow.

'And oh, Tom,' the Princess went on, 'do you have any milk on you? Because the Prince here hasn't drunk a thing for seven years, and he's feeling rather dry.'

'We finished the last of the milk,' said Tom, looking at their new companion in some wonderment, 'but what we do have is a bottle of ale.'

'Ale!' rasped the Hobgoblin, in a voice that spoke of dried-up wells, desert sands, and dying crops. 'A thimbleful—a drop only—would be worth half my kingdom!'

'Well, you're welcome to it,' said Tom, wondering what a goblin kingdom would be like. He passed it the bottle, and the Prince of Hobgoblins drank it down in a series of loud and luscious gulps. When it had finished, its face looked a bit less stiff and parched, and creaked into an ecstatic smile.

'My thanks to you,' said the Prince, in something more like a normal, squeaky goblin voice. 'Myself and my goblins are ever at your service.'

'That's very good to know,' replied the Princess affably.

'But how—' Tom began, still puzzling over how she had made the acquaintance of this queer personage.

'We escaped from a dungeon together,' said Princess Eleanor. 'And it was the luckiest thing that the jailer was mad keen on ballads, and I had with me a book I was going to give you to replace the one you lost—only now I can't, but I promise I'll get you another as soon as we're home. But what were you doing, charging about the passageways in such a careless manner?'

'It was the lodestone,' Tom replied, looking puzzled. 'I was trying to find the Enchanter so as to defeat him, but it seems the stone knew that what I really wanted most was to find you.'

'Well, that was handy of you,' replied the Princess, 'because the thing I most wanted was for you to find me.'

At that moment the Prince of Hobgoblins hissed at them to be silent, and pricked up its ears. 'Time is short,' the goblin rasped, 'and getting shorter. My ears are longer than yours, and have recovered much of their vigour thanks to your excellent ale. I can hear the comets dancing over the Castle, imps and impets fluttering up from their deep beds where they lie asleep like fallen leaves; ghosts are groaning from their graves, crying to be left to rest, but too weak to resist the Enchanter's imperious summons. I hear the tread of my own kind, bewitched to the Bold Enchanter's will, and the heavy tramp of the Sentinels. Your enemy fears you, and is calling all his minions to his aid. It is time either to confront the Enchanter, or make all speed from this Castle and hope to escape before his forces have time to gather.'

'Then we must seek him out,' cried Tom, and once again took up the lodestone in his fist. It almost jerked out of his hand, and the party set off at a brisk pace, with Tom in front. The way was dark, and from either side they heard sounds of scuttling and pattering and scratching, made by the beetles and spiders and earwigs that infested the lower regions of that cheesy keep. Some of them had been the Enchanter's enemies, and others had been servants he had used and then discarded, while others again were friends he had betrayed.

The lodestone pulled ever more strongly, and they were almost running when they turned a corner and pulled up short. Tom dropped the stone. Before them stood an enraged Sentinel, which swung its double-pointed halberd in the narrow space, bellowing out defiance, and frowning angrily from seven eyes.

The three retreated, and Eleanor whispered, 'What now, Tom?' while Tom was watching the giant carefully, probing for some weakness. Its mouth was opened very wide, with roars and threats pouring from it alternately. Tom reached into his haversack as the giant struck its halberd on the floor and challenged them to come on.

'You've got a very big mouth,' said Tom to the giant, holding something behind his back. 'This should fit in it very easily.' With that, he hurled a bottle between its enormous jaws. It gnashed its teeth with a crunch of broken glass, and the next moment stopped in amazement. Its weapon fell to the ground, every one of its eyes opened wide and round, and then it began to howl.

'Moonshine,' Tom explained, and the Princess hugged him delightedly. The goblin led them quickly around the bulk of the moonsick giant, who could only stare and howl and howl and stare, and Tom once more picked up the lodestone in his fist.

On they ran, now along many a dizzying stair that wound steeply upwards. The Castle was resounding with running feet and the call of trumpets, and the sighing and stirring of strange things, uncanny to hear. At last, they came out in the long passage that led to the Enchanter's private room. The great door at the end was barred by a Sentinel that looked more fierce and resolute than any before.

'You're going to say ''what now?'',' said Tom to Eleanor, 'and I don't know, because there's no more moonshine. We'll need a spell.'

But before he could begin to think of the words, there was a shrill cry of many voices, and from the shadows of the passage leapt a small army of goblins, who swarmed up over the giant, poking its many eyes and pulling its hair, rattling its halberd out of its grasp and untying its boots.

'My subjects!' shouted the Prince happily, and the goblins turned to the Hobgoblin with screams of joy.

'King of Pranks!' they called. 'Your Majesty is saved! Now the frolics and junkets will never, ever cease!'

It was that same band of goblins that had flown to the moon aboard the Eagle Inn. They had made their loyal way to the Enchanter's Castle to rescue the goblin Prince, knowing their duty by some instinct planted in them when they were no more than seeds.

The Sentinel was roaring now in pain and confusion, casting its eyes every way at once. It stumbled off down the passage, with goblins clinging all over it.

'What is your will, O Sire?' asked one of the goblins, jumping down.

'Force open that door,' replied the Prince, 'and then guard it. Our friends have business inside, and must not be disturbed.'

The goblins cheered, and on the Prince's command rushed at the door using the butt of the giant's halberd as a battering ram. The stout Cheddar planks gave way on the third try, and Tom and Eleanor advanced grimly into the Enchanter's den, the wand held between them.

CHAPTER 15

Moon Magic

The room now wore its true appearance. Mighty books of enchantments stood open on high lecterns, and candles guttered in the draught of the great bellows which fanned the several fires keeping the Enchanter's cauldrons on the boil. From these, the smell of scalding milk arose, mingled with the noxious scents of many harmful herbs. The Enchanter's Midget skipped about the room fetching this and that to add to the potions, shouting out the names of the things he wanted; and the jars and bottles, which bore no labels, answered when called.

And before them sat the Bold Enchanter himself, in the chair with its screaming armrests and the great wings folded behind its back, with the terrible portrait of Death beyond, the sight of which struck Tom and Eleanor with a chill.

As they came in, the Midget let out his wicked laugh, which spoke of crimes without number or chance of pardon, and the Enchanter stared at them with a look of surprise.

'I hardly expected to see you two again!' he said, with a mocking curl of his lip. 'My guards are very stupid, letting such a pair of lost children roam at large about my house, and you must have been quite clever, my boy, to rescue your little friend from her dungeon. But it was unlucky of you to try my patience twice.'

Then, without rising from his chair, he lifted his arms. In one hand he held a wand like Tom's, with which he made passes in the air as he began his spell:

'By the Fondue Mountain's cone,
by the ghosts that round me groan,
cage again my captive flown,
leave her friend to stand alone!'

There was a rattle and a clang, and bars of iron sprang from the floor and wrapped the Princess in a cage whose door slammed and locked itself upon its prisoner. Eleanor let out a cry of alarm, while the Enchanter smiled and began to chuckle.

'And now, my dear young man, are you fond of insects? Because you are about to become one.'

Tom looked in horror at Princess Eleanor, stretching her arms out through the bars, and felt the stab of loneliness which the Enchanter had hidden in the folds of his spell. Then the words of Cheesecrown came back to him: a wand of power, a level head, and a ready wit would be the Bold Enchanter's downfall. The wand was in his hand. His calm returned, and the words of a spell formed in his mind.

'Moon-bred mists and impets' whirr,
let the Princess be made free:
and the cage you made for her
now instead imprison thee!'

At once, the bars unwound themselves and grew down into the floor with a whine of metal and a rattle of locks, while in the same instant strips of iron shot up like ranks of wheat around the Enchanter's chair, growing over him until he was imprisoned fast. He let out a snarl of rage and surprise, and leapt forward off his chair, only to come up against the bars, which he gripped in frenzy.

'I'll punish you! I'll punish you! You'll soon see what

it is to dabble with spells in the very halls of the Bold Enchanter!' His hands made passes in the air, and a new enchantment began.

'Pow'rs of Moon and darksome night,
phantoms, spectres, ghouls, and ghosts,
fill my foe with deadly fright,
imps and impets thronged in hosts!'

A confused sound came from outside the Castle, followed by a chill rush of air into the room. Strands of icy mist blew all about, and clung fast to Tom, each one a shred of some life long past; one took his hand, another put its pale arm about his shoulders, so that the damp settled into his bones. Voices whispered in his ears, telling him of griefs that could never be comforted and wrongs done in life which could never be made good after death. The sad spectres stood over him and laid claim to him, and then the Enchanter's imps swept in like a storm cloud. They screamed in his face, and brushed all round like a swirl of dead leaves whipped up by the angry wind of early winter. The smaller ones of their kind, the impets, crept up close to his skin like leeches, or buzzed in his ears like untiring flies.

The Enchanter laughed, and cast a spell to remove the cage from around his chair, while Eleanor stared in dismay at the cloud of moving forms that shrouded Tom from her sight. He needed her help, but now that they were in their enemy's very den, she had no faith in her spells without the wand. She darted forward into the squirming mass of misty limbs that embraced and bore down on Tom's fainting body; voices whispered warnings to her, but she felt for his hand and grasped both it and the wand.

'By the waxing of the moon,
by the starry meteors' tune,
banish hence the Enchanter's slaves,
send them back to haunt their graves.'

With a groan and a scream, the whole swarm of ghosts
and imps separated itself from Tom. With looks of fear
or anger or surprise, the ghostly faces melted away into
smoke, and the imps and impets blew out through the
window like waste paper, chattering and cursing.

The Enchanter's face was blank with astonishment,
but then he smiled again, and spoke.

'Moon and sun and sky and air!
You make quite a handy pair!'

Tom was still reeling from the ghosts, and Eleanor
had hold of his hand. She looked at him in anxiety, and
then she said, 'It's a spell!'

'No, by starlight, it is not,' resumed the Enchanter in
a smooth, false voice, and then he went on, casting a
venomous look straight at the Princess, 'Strike her
speechless on the spot!'

Princess Eleanor opened her mouth in alarm, but not
a sound would come out. Tom saw at once the
Enchanter's trickery, to disguise his spells with flattering
words, and then render them both dumb, and so unable
to work any more magic.

'Now, by cheese, my little man,' went on the
Enchanter, smirking confidently, 'let's wind up what we
began.'

Tom faced him angrily, and gripped the Princess's
hand.

'No, by Sev'n, Moon's magic sum,
let her speak and you be dumb!'

Eleanor's voice came back in a cry of relief, while the Enchanter shook his fists in silent fury. But before either of them could think of another spell to cast, Tom felt something whisked away from his side.

'I have his wand!' crowed the Midget, who had slipped around behind Tom and deftly removed it from his belt. 'Master, we've beaten them now!'

But the Enchanter was looking frightened, and had fallen back, speechless, among his books and potions.

'Then I'm the new King of the Moon!' shrieked the Midget. 'Not so bold now, my former master, and not so clever, my little visitors!' Tom and Eleanor stared in horror, as the Midget touched himself on the head with the wand. But then, instead of the sense of power and mastery he had been expecting to feel flowing through his body, the Midget suffered a very strange sensation, and stood staring, rooted to the spot.

At this, Tom suddenly laughed out loud. 'It's the wrong wand! That was the willow wand for finding the Lady of the Woods: we have the moon wand in our hands!'

'Of course we do! Oh, Tom, he'll be searching for years if he looks for her up here!'

Meanwhile, though, the Enchanter had been finding in his books other charms, which worked without the use of the voice. The pages turned by themselves, and the words and figures he sought for shone out and spoke to him in quiet, silvery tones. In a moment, he was once more able to speak.

'Now, by Cheddar, we shall see
foe and traitor bow to me!'

Tom and Eleanor felt their necks forced forward into a bow, while the spellbound Midget curtsied nimbly;

and at the same moment the Princess completed the Enchanter's spell:

> 'And, by Edam, may your hands
> have the strength of desert sands!'

The wand fell from the Enchanter's grasp, and his fingers drooped weakly. He snarled with rage, and retreated again to his books, whose pages flapped and whose voices babbled with this spell and that.

'Tom, his books!' whispered Eleanor urgently. 'We must do something!'

Tom made no reply, but lifted the wand and began his enchantment.

> 'Thrice-filled pots of melted cheese,
> tubs of curds and butter pats,
> bring th'Enchanter to his knees,
> drown his books in milky vats.'

With a wail of despair, the Bold Enchanter sank to his knees. His lecterns stood around him, the books too high for him to read, and his wand lay useless at his feet. Then, with a rustle of pages and a hiss of frightened voices, the books rose up and floated across the room to the several cauldrons which still steamed and simmered on the fires. The spells cried out to their master to be saved, and some of the books tried to cast enchantments on their own account; but before any words of power could be said, one by one the Enchanter's books sank beneath the surface of the various bubbling potions. The inky letters were unloosed from their places and floated free in a confusion of noise, each syllable crying out as it was separated from its fellow, and then falling silent, drowned in the seething brew.

The Enchanter watched in agony as his books left

him, and now turned in rage to Tom and Eleanor. His eyes narrowed, and he began to mumble so low as not to be heard. He was still a sight to daunt his enemies. But Eleanor gripped Tom's hand, raised the wand once more, and spoke the last spell, the last enchantment to end all others.

> 'Moon, wherein th'Enchanter dwells,
> end his reign, undo his spells;
> turn his Sentinels to cheese,
> break his wand and steal his keys.'

The ground beneath their feet gave a heave and a shudder, as if the Moon herself had at last revolted against the magician who had held her so long in thrall. A shiver passed through the air, as every spell the Enchanter had ever cast was undone, every knot of his magic untied, every web unwound, and every enchantment unsung. The seven Sentinels hardened back into the cheese they had been before their master gave them life; the jars and bottles around the room groaned and fell silent; on the great chair the wings drooped and shrivelled, and the mandrakes on its arms shrieked in their death-throes. The wand at the Enchanter's feet snapped in two with a sound like the breaking of iron, and a bunch of many keys flew from his side and landed at the feet of the victors.

Then, the greatest of his enchantments began to unravel, and the Enchanter himself started to change. His hands, already weak, shrivelled into his sides; his dark cloak paled and faded to grey and then to white, and his frightened face receded into his neck, while his hair whitened and clung to his scalp, and in a few seconds his whole body was transformed to that of a great worm. Tom and Eleanor clung to each other and fell back from the writhing creature, staring in horror. But there was no longer any danger. They were seeing the Bold Enchanter in his true shape now, helpless and blind. The great worm twisted its body this way and that a few times, then set itself to tunnelling into the floor of the room, and in a few seconds more it was gone.

They both let out their breaths, and began to feel very shocked and tired and relieved. Then a great wailing and sighing rose up from all round the Castle. They rushed to the window, and saw a mighty concourse of ghosts gathering from every side, and flocking off in companies. Some were laughing and others were weeping, and a few were even singing; but who could tell what those spirits thought or felt as they were at last released from their master's thrall, and sped back to resume the broken rest of their graves?

The misty cavalcade passed over the rim of the Mountains, and a great silence settled over the Castle of the Bold Enchanter.

CHAPTER 16

Down to Earth

Tom and the Princess stood side by side and stared out through the window over the Cheddar Mountains, until they were startled by the sound of the doors being thrown open, and a gaggle of goblins entered the room.

'My friends!' burst out the Prince of Hobgoblins, his whole pimply face one enormous smile. 'You have overthrown the Bold Enchanter, and done what none before has even dared to try. And now you are master and mistress of his Castle.'

'I suppose we are,' agreed Tom, taking up the keys from the floor. 'And we'd better go round and make sure that all's well. But first we must find the wand.' The lodestone led him to a great chest in a corner, locked by seven keys. Tom unlocked each in turn, and inside they found the goblin horn, which the Prince of Hobgoblins had used in the old days to summon his subjects, and beside it the wand of the Lady of the Woods, light and green, and speaking of fragrant woods and summer air.

Then Tom and Eleanor went round the whole Castle. Everywhere they found hordes of creatures milling about in surprised delight. The goblin guards tore off their armour and frisked along the passages, Moonmen blinked their round eyes and wept to see their true forms restored, while here and there stood a silent Cheddar statue with seven walnut eyes, all that was left of the unsleeping Sentinels.

At last they all gathered in the courtyard, crossed the steaming moat, and began to make their way down the jutting Cheddar crag to the plateau. At the foot of the crag Tom and Eleanor recognized a familiar group: it was the knights, and they were having an argument. Nearby stood another pair of Sentinels frozen in defiant attitudes, one with a lance stuck through its body, and the other with its head missing.

'And I say it's the worst of bad manners to cut off your foe's head after he has been turned to cheese,' insisted Sir Politesse.

'And I say it's mine, and it's a trophy,' retorted Sir Vortigern hotly. 'Dozens of my ancestors did the same.'

'That hardly surprises me,' Sir Politesse sniffed.

'Hurry up,' put in another familiar voice. 'Hate hold-ups. Quick work, that, Vorty, turning 'em to cheese: never knew you had it in you. But best get on now, eh?'

At that moment the knights caught sight of the great army that was filing its way down to them from the crag above, and Sir Vortigern turned to Tom and Eleanor.

'Fair Princess, and worthy sir,' he said with a bow, still holding the surprised head of the Sentinel in his hand. 'As you see, gallant deeds of errantry have here been performed; allow me to lay the monster's head at Your Highness's feet as a token of humble devotion.'

He laid the grimacing face on the ground, and Eleanor eyed it with distaste. 'You're very kind, but why don't you keep it? And there isn't any more errantry to be done, because we've done it all. Why don't you come with us back to the inn, and we'll tell you all about it?'

So the puzzled knights joined in the great procession, which wound its way up to the darkened ridge of the Cheddar Mountains, and then down into the sunlit Emmenthal valleys. The wild hillmen watched from their caves, but did not dare attack so large and cheerful a company.

Before long they were down on the Plain, and ahead they saw the cheese-built town of the Moonmen, with the old oak inn nearby. As they approached, a great number of Moonmen surged forward, their hoods thrown back and their silver faces shining with joy. Long-lost friends were embraced and stories exchanged, and seven cheers rang out for the saviours of the moon. Then Cheesecrown made his way towards them, and the crowd fell back.

'Noble friends,' he said, taking their hands, 'I have ordered the rarest of banquets to celebrate your return. We shall have our cheese smoked, toasted, frozen, salted, grated, and grilled; and the central dish will be cheese fondue!'

Tom and the Princess looked at each other, and then they both spoke at once.

'Much as we appreciate the honour—'

'We really should get back—'

'Parents who worry—'

'So very kind—'

Cheesecrown nodded sadly, and called for another seven cheers. When the last cheer had died away, the Eagle unfurled its wings and gave a piercing screech, and Master Richard stepped from the door of the inn.

'We're bound for Earth: all Moonmen ashore!' Then he caught sight of the knights. 'Sir Vortigern! Are you sailing with us?'

'Nay, I think not,' replied the knight. 'If I understand aright, none of us has proved worthy of the hand of the fair Princess. It is our intention to remain on the moon. There are causes to fight for, the peaceful miners of the

Plains to defend from the wicked hillmen, and who knows what quests to go on besides.'

'And we'll teach these Moonmen to brew ale and make punch,' whispered Sir Dizziwind to Sir Bivouac, 'as soon as possible!'

With that, the knights gave Tom and Eleanor a salute or a bow, each in his own style, and turned back to the town, where the Moonmen were already gathering for the banquet. Princess Eleanor watched the knights out of sight, and heaved a huge sigh of relief.

'And if you please,' said a hoarse voice from the innkeeper's side, 'I'd like to beg a passage for myself and my subjects. They're a rough lot, but I'll answer for their behaviour on the voyage.'

Master Richard turned to find the Prince of Hobgoblins looking up at him. Almost the last thing he wanted in his inn was an army of goblins, but the Prince had stood firm by his friends, so he took the creature at its word, and the goblin host swarmed aboard.

Tom and Eleanor took their last steps on the springy Edam Plain and felt wooden boards beneath their feet once again. Goblins were told off into watches and scampered up to the garrets or out over the gallery, and now the Eagle stretched its wings out to the full. Oaken feet and talons uncurled beneath the building; another scream tore through the sky, and, with a powerful beat of its wings, the Eagle took off.

The goblins cheered and ran madly down the corridors, but Tom and the Princess looked out of the window in silence as the yellow plain fell away below them, and the Eagle set its course for the Earth. Both were thoughtful. From time to time one of them reminded the other of some adventure they had shared, and then conversation lapsed. Tom felt strangely sad as he thought of home, and how soon he would be parted from the Princess.

'Do you remember how you nearly drank from the pool of moonshine?' he asked after a while. 'And then you said you wanted a house beside a babbling stream, and you'd drink from it whenever you wanted, and never have any more milk or cheese.'

'I *would* like a house like that,' replied the Princess dreamily; 'somewhere just on the edge of the woods. It must be nice to live by a mill, and always hear running water.'

'It is nice,' agreed Tom, 'but the woods can be lonely too. The river sounds as if it's talking to you, but it's not.' He heaved a deep sigh, and the Princess looked up with a secret smile, which Tom did not see.

The meteor reefs and beaches of stardust were behind, the sky was tinged with blue, and the highest clouds began to streak past the inn, when the goblin look-outs let out a cry of 'Ship ahoy!'

Ahead was a bright blur like a cloudburst, coming towards them with no fixed outline. Around it moved dancing sparks of light like fireflies, and as they came closer the sparks resolved themselves into tiny winged creatures, which darted up to the windows of the inn and away again. Goblins clustered at the windows, beating their tails in excitement, and jumping back with a howl when one of the creatures came up close. In another moment, the burst of light swept into the inn, and where before there had been a bare wall, there now stood a handsome writing-desk, its many drawers, flaps, and hatches concealing the house of the Lady of the Woods. The front flap of the desk was lowered, and the Lady herself stepped from an inlaid door.

Her radiance flickered, as if between hope and despair, and all she said was, 'Do you have it?'

Tom came forward from the window-seat and held out the wand.

'Throw me it,' said the Lady, and Tom tossed the wand to the tiny creature. It turned in the air, shrinking as it came, and when it landed in her hand it balanced perfectly.

'And the Enchanter defeated,' she added, with a smile which warmed them like the sun on a summer's day. 'For now, farewell: work needs to be done!'

With that, the Lady of the Woods went back into the desk, and her carriage emerged from one of its pigeonholes; the dragonflies whirred and the whip sang with a voice hardly to be heard, and the coach flew swiftly across the room and out of the window. Tom and Eleanor watched it dwindle from sight as it glided down through the clouds, and then they both felt suddenly very tired. The moon, just waning from its full, was setting in the west, and dawn was coming to the Earth below. Their job was done. They each leant into a corner of the window-seat, watching the Earth rise slowly up to meet them, taking on more colour as the sun rose and the haze parted, and soon they were fast asleep.

Some time later, when the sun was up and casting its early light on the towers of the Castle, the Queen rose from troubled dreams. She yawned and got out of bed, and sat down at her dressing table to face her usual morning ordeal. She gave the grumpy comb a prod, but it didn't complain. She picked it up; it did nothing to resist. Then the Queen caught sight of a small, glossy apple, where yesterday there had been the uncanny bar of lemon soap. Joyfully, she opened all the drawers, pulled the lids off every pot, brushed her hair and grinned in the mirror.

'It's gone!' she shouted. 'The Magic and Mystery has gone!'

Other similar cries could be heard from all over the Castle. The Lord Chamberlain found that the Crown Jewels were no longer clamouring to be let out of their strongroom; the Head Cook sat and wept when he was told the hens were laying normally again, and the jester led Lady Clara to the door of the Queen's bedchamber, both their faces swimming in smiles.

The goblins ran through the Castle in a flustered state, and forgot to play their usual pranks. Then, just about breakfast-time, a cry sprang up among them that was repeated all over the Kingdom.

'Did you hear it?'

'Yes, I heard it!'

'He's back! He's back! He's back!'

They rushed off all together, and in seconds not a single one was left in the Castle. Breakfast was served in the Royal breakfast parlour with no din of capering goblins, no footmen called in to pursue them, and no fights between quarrelsome egg-cups. Peace and quiet had returned, but the King and Queen could hardly touch their food.

'Where, oh where, is our Princess?' moaned the Queen. 'And what, oh what, is happening?'

Just then, a shout was heard from the courtyard. A messenger had arrived at the Castle, after riding hard. He was sent straight up to the King and Queen.

'If it please Your Majesties,' panted the messenger, 'the Eagle Inn has been seen flying low over the hills to the west, and it looks as if it's going to land in its old spot.'

At once, breakfast was abandoned, and the whole court rode out after the bewitched building in which, it was said, Princess Eleanor had been spirited away on a journey no one knew where.

The last part of the flight had been slow and easy, just as when a fair wind wafts a ship-load of weary mariners to their home port, or when an old horse makes its way back to the stable it knows, while the rider nods in the saddle. As the Eagle flew in low over the hills, with the rising sun straight ahead, the Prince of Hobgoblins went up to the highest garret and blew its horn. Throughout the length of the Kingdom goblins pricked up their long ears to listen, and ran in the direction of the sound with joyful whoops.

The Eagle lowered itself at last over its old foundations; the oaken feet bent to soften the shock, and the cellar steps once again met the cellar below. It gave one last screech, folded its wings and fell silent, and the old oak post by the door of the inn has never again been known to move or utter a sound from that day to this.

Tom and Eleanor were shaken awake by the gentle jolt of the landing. They looked out to see a huge crowd of goblins thronging the village streets and the fields around. The Prince of Hobgoblins stepped out of the door of the inn, and a shrill and ear-shattering cheer rang out from thousands of goblin throats. The Prince held up its leathery hand, and said:

'My subjects, the thanks of all goblins are due to the two humanfolk who saved me from our enemy, and delivered all goblinkind from the Enchanter's power: the brave Sir Tom and Princess Eleanor!'

The goblins let out a yell, and a small band of them rushed up to the chamber over the front and dragged Tom and Eleanor out with them, bemused and protesting.

When they appeared at the door, the goblins cheered more wildly than ever, they lashed their tails and stamped their feet, and a goblin dance of triumph was just beginning when a trumpet sounded close by, and all fell silent.

There on the other side of the mass of goblins, the King and Queen sat on horseback, with around them their courtiers, footmen, ladies-in-waiting, and guardsmen. The goblin ranks fell back suspiciously, and then their Prince called out, 'Come, my subjects! Let us leave these humanfolk to talk of weighty things. We're off for the fields, and a grand goblin dance.'

A great whoop went up, a song began, and the whole body of goblins swept out of the village stamping out the rhythm, with their Prince at their head.

'My dear Eleanor!' cried the Queen, dismounting and rushing forward. 'Where can you have been? Were you stolen away? Where has all the magic gone? Which brave knight was the one who got rid of it?'

Tom was still standing uncertainly by the Princess's side, and Eleanor now took hold of his hand. 'It was Tom who did it,' she said, 'and we're to be married. We've talked it over and it's all settled.'

The Queen gave her a look of amazement which was only matched by the one Tom was giving her at the same moment.

'What's this, my dear?' asked the King, coming up with some courtiers and attendants.

'Our daughter says she is going to marry this . . . this person!' shrieked the Queen, while Tom was whispering hard to the Princess, who still gripped his hand.

'But we haven't talked it over at all,' he protested.

'Of course we have,' replied Princess Eleanor. 'On the way down in the inn, remember? You did beat about the bush rather, but I knew what you meant. And anyway, you've won me: don't forget the Proclamation.'

'Is this true?' put in the King. 'Did you indeed dispel the Magic and Mystery, my boy?'

'No,' replied Tom in a fluster. 'Not all by myself, anyway: Princess Eleanor did at least half the work, and she can't deny it.'

'I certainly can,' replied the Princess hotly. 'You had the courage to begin, and that's much more than half the battle. No one but you would have dared to look for the Lady of the Woods or fly to the moon. I just went along to keep an eye on you.'

'But you saved me from being eaten by the spider,' put in Tom, 'and from the ghosts and imps.'

'Well, you stopped me from drinking the moonshine,' pointed out Princess Eleanor, 'and you saved us both from the Enchanter's spells. Besides, you took all those risks for my sake, and if I did help a bit, that only means I've won your hand as well as you winning mine.'

The Queen was all at sea, tossed between bafflement and indignation and relief. 'I want to hear what Sir Vortigern has to say,' she burst out at last. 'Where is he? I really can't believe that—'

Her daughter smiled sadly and pointed at the sky.

'What do you mean? Where are our gallant knights?'

'They're still on the moon,' said the Princess drily. 'They didn't want to come back once they'd failed to win my hand, and good riddance. Tom's worth more than the batch of them boiled in a stew.'

'But, Michael,' the Queen moaned, plucking at the King's sleeve, 'he's just a common boy! And the Proclamation did say "to the brave *knight* who rids the Kingdom of Magic and Mystery"!'

'That, at least, is easily dealt with,' replied the King,

who drew his sword and ordered Tom to kneel. 'I dub thee Sir—what is your name, my boy?'

'Tom, Your Majesty,' replied Tom in wonder.

'I dub thee Sir Tom,' the King continued, touching Tom's shoulders with the sword, 'knight of the realm and protector of the innocent. Rise, Sir Tom!'

Tom stood up, and the Princess at once took possession of his hand again.

'And now, my dear,' said the King to the Queen, 'don't you think we should agree to the young people's wishes? That is,' he added, turning to Tom, 'if you are quite willing to take the reward specified in our Proclamation?'

'Oh, of course I am,' Tom assured him, covered in confusion, and holding Princess Eleanor's hand very tightly.

Then the Queen put on a brave smile and bustled forward towards Tom. 'Well, well, well,' she said. 'Everything's for the best, I'm sure. You must tell me all about your adventures when there's more time, Sir Thomas. I may call you that, mayn't I?'

'If Your Majesty pleases,' replied Tom in a daze.

'And you must call me "mother",' went on the Queen jovially.

'Very good—mother,' answered Tom.

Then the King turned to the courtiers and announced that Magic and Mystery were banished forever, and that Sir Tom was to marry the Princess Eleanor at the end of nine days' feasting. The village rang once more to the sound of cheers, when there was a rush of air, and the carriage of the Lady of the Woods drew up before the inn. She had made it grow to the size of a normal coach, and the courtiers' horses shied away from the great dragonflies which stood cleaning their faces and feet, their brilliant wings still throbbing. The Lady stepped down from the shining vehicle and curtsied gracefully to the King and Queen.

'Oh, I've been so foolish!' apologized the Queen. 'If only I hadn't wished for Magic and Mystery! If only—'

'Not at all,' interrupted the Lady of the Woods. 'It was not your wish that was at fault, but my wand; and now that my powers are restored, you are free to wish again, either for Magic and Mystery or for something else.'

The Queen looked taken aback. 'Oh, I don't think I will, thank you very much. I really think I have everything I need already. Perhaps the only thing I *didn't* have was the knowledge that there was nothing else I wanted.'

'Very well,' smiled the Lady. 'And I see our young people have come to an understanding. They have won each other, fairly and squarely, and I wish them joy!'

'And now,' said the King, 'let preparations be made for the feast!'

The trumpet again sounded, tables were set out in the fields, and the finest things from all the country around were brought together for the banquet. Barrels of the finest wine were broached, and people came flocking from the town and villages. Tom's parents and grandmother were sent for and seated at the King's table, and then, just as everyone was about to begin, a hoarse cheer was heard, and the goblins scampered forward. They would have swarmed everywhere, but their Prince called them to order and made them sit at a table of their own, where they called for ale and puddings and sausages and bread. Tom and the Princess were kept busy answering questions about their adventures; they tasted every dish that came before them, but when the cheeseboard was brought, they exchanged glances, and politely sent it away again.

At the end of the first day's feasting, the King stood up and made a speech. He decreed that Tom should be known as Prince Tom, and that together he and the Princess should rule over half the Kingdom, and then one day become King and Queen.

The people cheered three times for the King, three times for their new Prince and his bride, and then three times more just out of excitement. Healths were drunk and drunk again, and when the sun set there was dancing until dawn. Coloured lanterns hung in the trees, and those who wished could wander off into the woods, where paths wound along the hillsides and the river banks, and there were no longer any ghosts or spooks to frighten anyone.

When the nine days were at last at an end, Eleanor and Tom were married, and then everyone prepared to go their separate ways. The goblins kept up their feasting and dancing to the very last moment, and it was late on the ninth day when the Prince of Hobgoblins began to marshal his subjects. Dusk was falling, and Tom and Eleanor were strolling between the emptying tables, when the goblin prince appeared by their side.

'My friends,' he said, and his voice was now more squeaky and less raspy than ever, 'it's time we goblins said farewell. We go to a far-off land, out of the way of humanfolk, where goblins can be goblins, and the frolics and romps can go on and on forever. But we're your friends for good, and if ever you're in need of us, you have only to seek us out.'

The Prince of Hobgoblins faded into the shadows, and a few moments later the note of a horn drifted out over the hills and the valley below. There was a sound of scuffling and scampering, and squeaks and howls, and then a goblin song drifted up from the plain as the army set off, and the last of the Queen's Magic and Mystery left the Kingdom.

Dusk was falling deeper than ever, and Tom and Eleanor wandered off hand in hand along the path into the woods. Bats swooped and fluttered down almost into their faces, and a raucous croak rang out along the valley as the dark shape of a heron flapped slowly downstream for the night. Owls began to call and answer each other from this side and that. Eleanor clung to Tom's arm and looked to see where the sounds had come from.

'Are you sure these woods aren't still enchanted?' she asked.

The moon was rising in the east, and a silvery light began to play on the bubbling waters of the river. Tom smiled.

'Well, maybe they are,' he admitted, and they walked on together in the darkness.

GALWAY COUNTY LIBRARIES

Also by Weem Whitaker

The Alchemy Set

ISBN 0 19 271767 7

You can't change the ending just by working magic. Or can you?

When Charlotte and David finish reading their book, they are horrified at the unhappy ending. The prince is lured to his death, and of course there's nothing they—the readers—can do.

But the alchemy set changes all that. When Charlotte and David realize it can work magic, they decide to conjure up the world of the book and go in to warn the prince. But it's not as easy as all that. And when they get into the world of the book, they find things are different. Whom can they trust? Who is real? And will they reach the prince in time?

'an action-packed adventure'
School Librarian